I0546197

80'S
BABY

WHEN CRACK MADE KINGS

80'S BABY

BABY

WHEN CRACK MADE KINGS

TY MARSHALL

80's Baby : When Crack Made Kings

Copyright © 2015 by Ty Marshall.

The Official Writers League™ and all associated logos are trademarks of The Official Writers League LLC.

All rights reserved. Printed in the United States of America. No part of this book may be used or reproduced in any manner whatsoever without written permission except in the case of brief quotations embodied in critical articles or reviews.

This book is a work of fiction. Names, characters, businesses, organizations, places, events and incidents either are the product of the author's imagination or are used fictitiously. Any resemblance to actual persons, living or dead, events, or locales is entirely coincidental.

For information contact :

www.tymarshallbooks.com

Book Cover design by Oddball Dsgn & Josh Wirth
ISBN: 978-0-9984419-1-7

First Edition: December 2016

10 9 8 7 6 5 4 3 2 1

"EITHER YOU SLINGING CRACK ROCK OR YOU GOT A WICKED JUMP SHOT."

— BIGGIE

PROLOGUE

Papo stood looking out into the clear New York City night. From his position on the roof, he swore he could see the flicker of the lights from the Manhattan skyline. He had taken in the view hundreds of times before but never had it seemed so vivid like it did on this night. Just a little over a year ago he laid in a jail cell thinking of this exact moment. Now here he was, perched atop the largest projects in The Bronx, literally and figuratively. But he couldn't enjoy it, at least not right now, time was of the essence and he kept checking his pager every few minutes as his impatience grew with each passing second. He had begun to get antsy thinking that the person he had been waiting on wouldn't show at all. He reached in his pocket, removing a pack of cigarettes and sparked up a Newport, the third one in the past 20 minutes. He took a long pull on the cancer stick causing the tip to steam before exhaling a cloud of smoke into the night air, trying his best to calm his nerves and ease the anxiety he felt. Papo was a ball of energy, but it was good energy though. The kind a child experiences on Christmas morning as they stare at the presents under the tree, ready to start ripping at the wrapping paper. Chain smoking Newport's wasn't working, so he tossed it to the ground and snuffed it out with his foot. Reaching into his waistline he removed his gun, a stainless steel Beretta 9 and popped out the clip, checking to make sure it was full before pushing it back into place. Just gripping the steel in his hand made him feel like a God and he couldn't have been any closer to the clouds scattered across the night sky than he was right now. Hearing the door to the rooftop open behind him, he quickly turned with the gun raised, feeling flushed with invincibility as he stood atop the Edenwald projects with the moon at his back. Just like the Gods in Greek mythology thought that eating certain fruits gave them eternal life, Papo's sense of immortality came from the three-day crack binge he was on currently. Blinded with desperation, he had reached the point where he was willing to do anything to get more cash to cop more crack. The euphoric rush it gave him was a fleeting high, lasting for only 10 minutes. Then it would be replaced by overwhelming sadness, erasable only by another blast. He was like a dog chasing a mechanical cat in a circle. He once controlled the swarm of marauding crack addicts that flooded the projects in search of their next hit. But he was now a slave to the little white rock himself. It controlled his every thought and he followed its every command. What started out as a whisper quickly became a loud booming voice in his head telling him to do the once unthinkable. Papo had turned his gun on Hassan, the man he once called his brother. The two had fought many street wars back to back and had gotten hood rich together but their bond had been eroded by addiction and greed.

For the residents of the Edenwald Houses, Hassan's crew operations had become the only normalcy they knew. Drug deliveries were more reliable than the mail and gunfire was a constant. Life in Edenwald was like living in a one factory town,

Hassan was the boss and everybody wanted to work for his crack company. On rooftops, in hallways and behind closed doors of apartments, people of all ages were in on some part of the action. Kids transported drugs and cash in their book bags for new sneakers and spending money hoping to gain enough respect to be invited into the crew's inner circle. Women bottled crack at their kitchen tables and stored it in closets and under mattresses, along with guns and cash, in order to live rent free. The money was too good for most people to resist. Hassan had truly built himself an empire. The name Major Coke Movers, rang throughout the Bronx. It derived from the large amount of cash they were making, $350,000 a week with as many as 2,000 customers a night coming through the projects. Members of the team sported MCM rings and gold belt buckles signifying their membership.

One look into Papo's eyes and Hassan could only see the devil staring back at him, along with the gun in his hand. There were no remains of his former comrade left, crack had made him a shell of himself. He saw the dark circles and the sunken in face as Papo's beady eyes darted back and forth as sweat poured down his face and he couldn't find a way to stay still, fidgeting constantly. Sadly, Hassan had noticed some of the signs that Papo had been getting high before tonight but he chose to ignore it. He really pushed the thoughts out of his mind, hoping they weren't true, just products of his own paranoia of being the king on the throne. Staring down the barrel of his unstable friend's gun, he deeply regretted not checking his homeboy about his suspicions.

"Yo, whatchu doing?" he questioned seeing the gun pointed at him. "Look 'atchu, you buggin' B," Hassan said watching his lifelong friend unravel right before his eyes.

"Nah I ain't buggin' god," Papo explained speaking the language of the Five Percent Nation, the religion he had adopted while serving time in jail. "This is the way it has to be. I'm tired of rocking in your shadow. This my hood too," he said pointing over to the forty buildings that made up Edenwald. Their crew controlled them all.

"You right B," Hassan acknowledged.

Together they had risen to the top of the crack game, Hassan had done what was said to be impossible. Uniting the north and south sides of the projects as one and it made them rich but more importantly it had made him a street legend, just like the hustlers they grew up hearing stories about and admiring. Niggas like Rick Rude from Gun Hill projects, Puerto Rican Primo from Boston Road, El Jefe, Shank from Castle Hill and Georgio and his De La Crème crew from Soundview, all Bronx cats that had legendary runs. But now it was them, they had the streets going crazy.

"You right but this ain't you, this ain't us baby," Hassan tried reminding his friend. He wasn't built to bend or beg and he refused to do either, not even for his own life. He didn't feel in fear of Papo, who was clearly on the edge. What he felt in his heart was more like sorrow. He was sorry for what the game had done to their once inseparable friendship and he regretted what crack had done to his friend. Papo was dangerous, he was a fiend and a fiend couldn't be trusted. Hasan knew this, unlike a functional crack-head, a fiend would do anything to get their next hit including; lie, cheat, steal, and snitch or kill. Not the type of person you want in your organization. But Hassan had gambled on Papo and it had come up snake eyes.

"See there you go, thinkin' you know what's good for me. You not my boss nigga, you might run the rest of these bitch ass niggas out here but not me. I do what the fuck I want," Papo barked as spit formed in the corners of his mouth. His jaw twitching uncontrollably, swinging to one side like a typewriter as he talked.

"You Illin' B," Hassan said shaking his head with his hands in both pockets of his blue & red velour Fila sweatsuit. "Smoking that shit got your head all fucked up."

"Nah, I'm thinking real straight," Papo said steadying the gun in his shaky hand. "I'm thinking I'm tired of hearing Hass this, Hass that out here in these streets. It's time they start talking bout me. It's my time to shine. Show the streets how I get busy, you feel me? You old news," he boasted. Truth was he was talking big, trying to convince himself to squeeze the trigger, even in his desperate state he still had love for Hassan. They had too much history for him not to but cash was king on these Bronx blocks and Papo wanted it all for himself.

Tears began to form in the wells of his eyes as he reminisced about their origins. "You remember Hass, this is where it all started," he said in a more somber tone, tears now running down his face. "Right here on this roof, we said we would take over the city," he said no longer able to hold back the tears.

"And we did," Hassan interrupted him.

"Nah, you did," Papo spewed, his jealousy crystal clear. "This roof holds a lot of memories for us, good and bad. You remember right?" he asked nodding his head.

"Yeah I remember," Hassan said knowing exactly what his friend was referring to.

"It shoulda been you," Papo said as venom filled his veins and the rage return to his eyes. "You shoulda went away too, not just me. But I'm about to make all that right. The projects belong to me now, you fired," Papo announced.

Boom! The shot rang out hitting Hassan in the chest. Papo jumped back with a look of shock on his face as Hassan rushed towards him, grabbing at him trying to wrestle the gun out his hands. Boom! Papo fired again hitting him in the stomach this time. Hassan eyes opened wide, staring at his friend in disbelief as the light in them began to dim and life quickly left his body as he collapsed to the ground.

For a moment, it almost seemed unreal; Papo couldn't believe what he had done. Watching Hassan's body crumble to the ground sent him into panic mode. "Oh shit," he said as he paced back and forth franticly with his hands on his head and tears streaming down his face, the gun still warm in his palm. "Fuck!" he shouted. "My bad Hass, I'm sorry B, I swear," he continued talking into the air, hoping his friend's soul could hear his apology. Finally, he composed himself then stood over Hassan's body and began going through his pockets, removing a knot of cash out of one of them. The gleam of the gold and diamond pendant that hung from the rope chain around Hassan's neck caught Papo's greedy eyes. It was covered in blood but even that couldn't dull its shine. The lion head piece was the talk of the town, all the women admired it and all the stick up kids dreamt of lifting it off his neck. It symbolized his power, he was the king of the concrete jungle. Papo now wore that crown and needed the streets to know it. He snatched the chain off of Hassan's lifeless body, then jetted for the door that led to the steps, leaving his former friend with his life leaking out on to the gravel beneath him. Ending his reign where it all began.

CHAPTER ONE

HASSAN 1980

"Nuffin' betta than the summer time in the city," Samantha said then took another swig from her can of Olde English 800.

"Yo, fa'real right?" Hassan said as he looked over the side of the building and down into the courtyard at the people going in and out of the building. "I love my hood; I can't see me ever leavin' here. I know everybody, the gangstas, the old ladies in the windows and the junkies and they all know me. Why would I ever want to go anywhere else?" he stated tossing his empty can across the rooftop. His smooth dark brown skin blended in with the night sky but his green eyes seemed to glow in the dark making it impossible not to stare at him. Wearing a white Polo shirt, shorts and shell top Adidas, his style of dress didn't set him apart from any of the other teenage boys running around the projects. It was his demeanor that towered over the others. He had a quiet confidence about himself that even at his age made people want to follow him.

Hassan and Sam, as she was called, weren't exactly dating but the two 16 year olds acted like it. They ran in the same circle and secretly Hassan had taken her virginity. Sam was a prettier than average, caramel complexion, young tender with a lot of ass and sass to match. She wore her hair in a ponytail with the baby hairs laid neatly along the edges and a blue tube top with a pair of cut off jean shorts. She lived off Schieffelin, near Baychester projects but spent the majority of her days ripping and running through Edenwald with a few of her home girls. Just like most teenage girls, she loved to break the rules set for her at home and frequently cut school, snuck up on the roof with Hassan and his crew to smoke reefer and drink beer.

"Not me," she replied. "I can't wait to get out of here," she stated, walking over and standing next to him. She placed her hand on his back and rubbed it in a circular motion.

"Where you going?" Hassan asked as if to say he didn't believe she had anywhere else to go, just like him and the rest of the kids stuck in the slums. He couldn't see himself anywhere else, instead he promised to make the best out of a bad situation. Hassan had plans on being the man, his street dreams weren't as far fetch to him as it might have been to others. His grandfather once ran a section of Harlem and would often share stories of his glory days with Hassan. He soaked it all in and had long decided his path in life.

"Anywhere but here," Sam answered. "I don't wanna be like all the girls around here, pregnant, on welfare with a section 8 apartment in one of these buildings. You know Keisha Maxey's grandmother lived here her whole life. And when she died, Keisha's mother took over her apartment and when she dies Keisha probably gonna do the same thing. It's a never ending cycle."

"That's some bugged out shit," Hassan said with a chuckle.

"Exactly," she shouted. "That's all you got to look forward to staying around here."

"Nah, I got big plans," Hassan proclaimed.

"And what's that?" she asked.

"You'll see," he said smoothly then turned looking back out over the building while cracking open another beer.

"That's the last one?" Sam asked.

"Here, you can have it. Papo on his way up with some more as we speak. I just seen him come in the building wit' ya girl."

About five minutes had passed when Papo and Ebony, one of Samantha's home girls, walked through the door on the roof.

"Yo," Papo shouted holding the six pack of beer in his hand as he burst through the door. "I got some more brew," he announced.

Papo was a slim built Puerto Rican kid whose real name was Joselito. He and Hassan had been tight for as long as they could remember. Their mothers ran the streets together turning tricks and chasing their heroin fix, which left the two of them alone to run the streets themselves, unimpeded.

"My nigga," Hassan said with a smile on his face. 'What up Eb," he nodded.

"Hey Hass," she greeted.

"Did you get some herb?" Sam asked.

"You know it," Papo sung in a bit of a melody, pulling out a Ziploc bag full of marijuana.

"Roll up," Sam shouted tossing Papo a pack of EZ Wider.

Papo quickly obliged and before they knew it, they had two joints in rotation. Hassan didn't smoke, so he just sat back sipping beer while the other three elevated their minds. Papo took a long toke and blew out O rings with the smoke.

"Yo Hass, we need to step our shit up. This nickel and dime hustling shit ain't gonna get it. Selling nickel bags of weed ain't making us no money," Papo declared.

"It ain't making you no money," Hassan teased his friend. "I'm making money. You smoking your profit up. Can't hustle with a habit homeboy."

Papo bust out laughing, knowing his friend was telling the truth. "Either way, we need to start getting some real paper. Like Dopeman Dave and dem over on the Southside."

"Yeah, I heard dat. I'm working on something tho," Hassan informed.

"Ain't nobody just gonna give us something. We

gotta earn our stripes out here on these blocks." Papo boasted.

"I ain't looking for no handouts," Hassan quickly responded.

"Yo what was in that herb," Ebony said as she had begun to feel funny. She took off her shirt and then her pants, standing on the roof in just her panties and bra. "I'm on fire, I'm on fire," she began to shout and run around on the roof before stopping and rolling around as if to try and put out the fire.

"Yo! what's wrong wit' ya girl?" Hassan asked Sam. "Why she buggin out?"

"I don't know but I feel weird too. You know what kind of reefer you got us smoking Papo?" Sam questioned.

"That's angel dust," he said with a smirk on his face. "That's what you thirsty bitches get, always trying to smoke for free," he laughed loudly.

"Who you calling a bitch, you fucking spic," Sam shouted swinging her arms wildly at him before Hassan stepped in to break them up.

"Cool out," he said unable to stop himself from laughing.

"Da fuck you laughing for?" Papo asked with a menacing look in his eyes. He was a hot head who would snap at a moment's notice.

"Sam was about to wax that ass," Hassan answered still laughing as he held her back.

"Oh yeah," Papo said. "Let that bitch go, betchu I'll fuck her up," he shouted angrily towards her.

"You ain't gonna do shit, you all talk," she screamed feeling stronger than ever from the effects of the PCP running through her.

"Wanna bet," Papo said pulling a .32 snub nose revolver out his waist.

"Yo, what you gonna do wit that shit nigga? She a girl man," Hassan said. "That shit ain't cool pulling a gun on a female nigga. You trippin'," he told his friend. "Yo Sam, just get your girl and put her clothes on and y'all jet, we'll get up later," he said turning his back on Papo and facing her. The sternness in his voice made her obey his request. Hassan had a way with words, he was smooth yet firm and Sam moved quickly racing over to Ebony to help her.

"You the one trippin' man, you too soft on them hoes," Papo said as Hassan turned back to face him.

"Nah nigga that hot head shit gonna get you jammed up out here in these streets. You gotta start thinking before you react like dat," Hassan schooled his partner. "A nigga gotta be smart and ruthless to be a boss. A plain ol' ruthless nigga just becomes a solider."

Papo heard what Hassan was saying but he was still pissed at Sam for trying to get fly with him. "Yeah, yeah nigga, I hear you," he answered half-heartedly. He opened the gun and spun the chamber than slammed it back in place. He repeated that over and over trying to calm his nerves and after a while it seemed to work.

Sam picked up Ebony and began helping her put her clothes on. She managed to get her dressed than walked back over to Hassan to say goodbye. The effect of the drug hadn't hit her as hard as her friend and she was able to keep it together.

"I'm sorry for being an asshole," Papo said as she passed by him. The toying with the gun had calmed him down. "It was a bad joke, my fault."

Sam ignored him and stepped between him and Hassan, giving Hassan a hug. "Ok we leaving," she said. "I'll see you tomorrow."

"Bet," he answered. "Yo make sure you get your girl some milk on her stomach. I heard that helps calm that high."

"Ok I will, I can't believe I smoked some dust," she said slightly laughing.

"Yeah that's crazy right…"

Boom!

The sound of the gunshot made Hassan duck to the ground, not quite sure where it had come from. As he looked up, he saw a frightened look on Papo's face as he held a smoking gun in his hand.

"It…It just went off," he said stuttering as he spoke. "I didn't mean…"

Hassan looked over at Sam who was lying face down on the ground next to him with blood leaking from her head. She wasn't moving or making a sound.

"Oh shit," he mumbled to himself realizing what had just happened.

Ebony began to scream at the sight of her friend's dead body lying there.

"Yo shut the fuck up," Papo yelled at her. "Yo we gotta get outta here," Papo shouted to Hassan.

"We can't just leave her like this man," Hassan said.

"What the fuck we supposed to do? Stay here and wait for the cops," Papo said.

Hassan knew his friend was right but it felt wrong to leave Sam on the roof like that. But what was he supposed to do? Wait for the cops to come and try explaining the story? Hell no, he would be in cuffs and down at the 47th precinct in the drop of a dime. He rushed to his feet, took one last look at Sam and said, "C'mon we gotta get out of here."

Ebony hesitated to move and Papo turned his gun on her. "You could either leave with us or lay with her," he gave her the options. But it really was an easy choice. Ebony cooperated with the gun totting teen and raced towards the door with the two of them.

Ebony's cooperation wouldn't stop there, her guilty conscience ate at her for days. The thought of Sam's dead body lying there haunted her every waking moment. Finally, she broke and told her parents what had happened and a week later she walked into the police station and gave a full account of the events on the roof that night. The police picked up Papo within hours and charged him with manslaughter sending him to Spofford, the infamous facility for youth offenders. Hassan got lucky, he was never charged with anything and remained on the streets to put his plan in motion.

CHAPTER TWO

Hassan's weed hustle had expanded to the point where he had assembled a little crew of his own and along with the fat dime bags he had started selling weight. Making good on his promise to Papo to step his shit up, he had only wished his right hand man was there to see it. Hassan wasn't the type to go on jail visits or write letters but he made sure Papo kept money on his books. He also had different females sending letters and pictures upstate to the jail, hoping it would get him through his bid.

Out on the streets Hassan was making a nice piece of change every week from his growing weed business. His small crew consisted of a set of twin brothers nicknamed Twin and Birdie, they ran like a well-oiled machine, and they weren't taking shit off of anybody. Young or old it didn't matter Hassan would step to his business and handle it. His way of moving caught the eyes of some of the Bronx's most notorious hustlers and they all tried recruiting him into their crew. But he passed on the offers, instead waiting on the perfect opportunity to come his way. That opportunity came unexpectedly one night while searching for a nigga that had ran off with some money that belonged to him. Hassan felt the only reason the nigga had ran off, was because he assumed that Hassan being so young wouldn't do anything to him. Never one to get chumped, Hassan planned on making an example out of the older nigga when he caught up to him.

He had just gotten word that the nigga he was looking for had been spotted on the Ave posted up, out in the open like shit was sweet. That infuriated him, it was a blatant show of disrespect and it had to be dealt with. Hassan stalked up Laconia Ave with no mask or hood on. He wanted everybody to see who was responsible for what was about to happen. As he turned the corner he spotted his target right where they said he would be, in front of Wong's Chinese spot, engaged in a conversation with a female. Hassan pulled the gun from his waist, calmly walked up on him and struck him in the face with it. A nasty gash opened on the man's face as Hassan hit him again. The older hustler tried to run but his vision was blurred by the blood in his eyes causing him to stumble over some bags of trash piled up on the side walk. That was all Hassan needed, he was on top of him in seconds striking him repeatedly with the gun, every swing landing a crushing blow. The man crawled into the street as people rushed out of the Chinese restaurant and formed around them trying to see what was going on. Battered and bloody the man begged for him to stop but there would be no end in sight. Hassan was there to prove a point. He never even made a sound. As the crowd grew, so did his anger as he continued to pummel the man. Tired of playing Hassan cocked the gun and pressed it to the man's forehead and pulled the trigger but it jammed. He tried squeezing it again, still nothing. Pissed off, he lifted the gun up once again ready to hit the man in the face but was stopped in mid swing when the gun was snatch out of his hand. He turned around prepared to go at it with whoever had chosen to interfere in his business but stopped when he saw who it was. A 6'5, 300 pound Puerto Rican, with a long leather trench and dark shades on, that everybody in the hood knew as El Jefe's number one henchmen.

"Yo, somebody wants to speak with you," was all he said before stepping to the side.

Hassan immediately saw El Jefe's red BMW and after a few seconds of staring, he walked over to it.

"Hassan right?" El Jefe asked to which the young man nodded his confirmation. "Get in," the drug baron ordered. "Listen, if I wanted to kill you, my man right there would have put a bullet in your head already," he said seeing Hassan apprehension. "Now don't make me repeat myself."

Hassan opened the door and got in. The BMW burned rubber as it pulled off the block. El Jefe was known just as much for his fleet of expensive cars as he was for the coke he moved. He had built his empire on the quality of his blow and the level of brutality he displayed dealing with those that opposed his rise to the top. Word on the streets, he was making about a million dollars a week as one of the top suppliers in the city. As Hassan sat quietly in the car, he couldn't help but to think that this was the type of opportunity he had been waiting for.

"So what was all that back there about?" El Jefe said breaking the deafening silence in the car.

"That man took something that belong to me," Hassan stated.

"Must have been important," El Jefe said. "If the punishment fits the crime."

"Yeah, he ran off with my money and I needed him and everybody else to know how important my bread is to me," he replied.

El Jefe nodded his head admiring the young man's approach to business because it wasn't that much different from his. He had kept a close eye on Hassan, noticing his leadership skills and no nonsense approach to how he dealt with the other kids around the neighborhood. He was tough and didn't seem to be afraid of anything. El Jefe liked that and decided to ask around about him. He found out Hassan came from the bloodline of a well-respected gangster from Harlem's past. He knew then he wanted the young thoroughbred on his team.

"So how much was that beat down worth?" he asked wanting to know how much the dude had run off with.

"Two hundred dollars," Hassan said still upset about it.

"Two hundred dollars," El Jefe laughed from his gut. He would have sworn the man had beat him for a few thousand the way Hassan tried to kill him.

"It's not about the money," Hassan interrupted. "It's about principle, I can't have nobody thinking they can chump me off. You let one person get away with it you become free lunch."

El Jefe pulled over to the curb and stopped. "You got a good head on you and a lot of heart," he said. "You know anything about cocaine?"

"Nah," Hassan said shaking his head.

"Here's some advice kid, if anybody ever asks you if you know something about something. Never say no, always say a little bit. You may be closing the door on an opportunity," El Jefe explained. "Anyway if you're ever ready to make some real money, come see me," he told Hassan then peeled ten hundred dollar bills off of a knot and extended it to him.

"This should cover your loss plus."

Hassan waved off the gesture. "It's cool, your friendship is enough," he said extending his hand.

El Jefe's face grew a wide smile. "You sharp kid," he said putting the money back in the knot than shaking Hassan's hand. "I need somebody like you on my team."

Hassan stood stoic with his back pressed against the wall, tightly gripping the sawed off shotgun in his hand. From his position he could see the entire apartment and had a perfect line of sight to all the workers. Those workers, both men and women, stood over tables covered in mounds of some of the purest cocaine the city had to offer. The assembly line like operation was responsible for weighing and bagging every last flake. El Jefe wouldn't have it any other way.

After getting a job as a lookout at one of El Jefe's spots, Hassan wasted little time taking advantage of the opportunity, rising up the ranks quickly. His attention to detail and strategic thinking gained the boss's confidence and he soon became his favorite young guy on the team. El Jefe took him under his tutelage teaching him the operation from ground up. Every morning the two would eat breakfast together and discuss business. He began grooming Hassan to manage his own spot even though he was just a few months away from being 17. Hassan was placed inside the spot in Castle Hill called "The Table" because the boss wanted him to see all parts of how the operation worked but also because he wanted one of his best men keeping an eye on his coke. The fact that the

Puerto Rican drug dealer trusted the young black teenager was an amazing feat in itself because it was said that El Jefe didn't trust his own mother. He was suspicious of everyone in his organization and his paranoia drove his underlings crazy. They walked on egg shells never knowing when he would point his finger at them and order them to be killed. He created an atmosphere of fear and he loved it like that.

Hassan kept his eyes glued to the workers and watched as the coke on the table disappeared in a few hours only to be quickly replenished and the process repeated. Tired of standing in one spot, he began to circle the different tables set up in the apartment. Most of the workers didn't even look up to acknowledge his presence. They just continued bagging up the blow. As he approached another table, he noticed two Hispanic men talking amongst one another as they worked.

"Mira este idiota moreno," one joked to the other about Hassan causing them both to laugh.

"Que va hacer el cabronsito este con una pistola," the other man said. "Se lo meto por el culo yo mismo," threatening to stick Hassan's gun up his ass. The two had long been plotting on El Jefe. They had plans on killing him and Hassan.

"What he doesn't know is he won't be able to do shit soon," the taller of the two men spoke in Spanish to his partner. "El Jefe ya pronto no va hacer en cargo," he bragged.

"No puedo espera ponerle una bala en su maldita cabeza! Ese se cre que todo el mundo le tiene miedo, canto de pendejo," he said dying for the chance to put a bullet in El Jefe's head.

Hassan walked up on the two men. "What's so funny fellas? Let me in on the joke," he asked seeing the two Spanish speaking men enjoying a laugh.

"Look at the piece of shit," the tall Hispanic man said to the other one in Spanish causing him to laugh. "Nothing my fren," he said speaking in English to Hassan. "Just talking baseball, trying to make the time past," he lied. The two men hated Hassan, calling him a black dummy every chance they got.

"Yeah, that's all my fren," the other man said knowing Hassan had no idea what they had been saying.

"Yeah, you like the Yankees?" Hassan asked making small talk.

"Yeah, papa. Go Yankees," he shouted in his heavy accent.

"Yeah, Go Yankees," Hassan said with a smirk,

truthfully he could give two fucks about the Yankees or any sport for that matter. All he cared about was making money.

"Mierda para cerebros," the man said as Hassan walked away.

"Mierda para cerebros," Hassan repeated. The men once explained to him that what they were saying meant something friendly, but they actually were calling him shit for brains. He took his place back on the wall and resumed watching.

There was a knock on the door of the apartment and a large goon, with an even bigger gun, stood up from his stool, walked over to the door and looked through the peephole. After a few seconds the door swung open and El Jefe himself entered the apartment draped by two of his henchmen. The smooth cocaine king was dressed in a charcoal gray sharkskin suit and a black dress shirt with the top two buttons open. He wore a pair of black sunglasses and walked with the stride of a boss. He made his way around the room taking in his elaborate operation making sure everything was running smooth. Finally, he walked over to Hassan, leaned in and whispered something to him. Hassan listened, his face never changing while the man spoke. Then when it was his turned he leaned in and whispered something in returned.

"Lock it down!" El Jefe ordered as his voice boomed through the room startling all. His henchmen immediately dead bolted the door and made sure all the windows were completely covered. "I want everybody's attention," he spoke at a lesser tone now.

As everyone locked their eyes on the powerful man in the middle of the room, El Jefe called Hassan over to him. "Come here," he said waving his hand. Hassan walked over and stood next to the boss, who placed his hand on his shoulder. He shook Hassan playfully and smiled,

"Now tell them your secret," he instructed.

Hassan smiled then spoke, "Yo no solamente hablo espanol lo inteindo bien, yo se todo lo que ustedes dicen" he told them all. "I hear what you say about me and about El Jefe. Especially you two," he said to the shock of every worker in the spot. Hassan had learned to speak Spanish from years of being around Papo, his mother, and El Jefe had used it to his advantage placing the young man in the spot knowing his workers would speak freely around him.

"Good job," El Jefe said with a nod as a gesture of his approval. "Bring me those two," he instructed his henchmen who quickly grabbed the two men.

They were already begging for their lives by the time they were placed on their knees in front of him. El Jefe took the sawed off shotgun from Hassan and pointed it at the chest of one men who were plotting his demise. "Let this be a lesson to you all," he said before instructing one of his henchmen to crank up the music. Then he pulled the trigger blowing a gaping hole in the first man's head. He quickly turned the weapon on the other man who was crying and pleading for his life and squeezed, blowing the man's head into pieces sending fragments of his brain and skull, spraying all over the room. He handed the gun back to Hassan then headed for the door.

"Back to work everyone," he said as his henchmen opened the door for him to exit.

Hassan stared down at the two dead bodies at his feet. It wasn't his first time seeing someone killed, so instead of being horrified by the massacre, he took a mental note of how to deal with disloyalty if it should ever rear its ugly head at him. More importantly he had foiled a plot and saved the life of one of the most powerful men in the street, a deed that wouldn't go unnoticed by El Jefe.

CHAPTER THREE

The beeping of the heart monitor and sound of the SERVO 900 ventilator pumping breathable air into the elderly man's weak lungs, created a rhythmic melody as they worked in unison preserving the little life he had left. At 72, his once strong body was quickly failing him, suffering two heart attacks and a stroke in less than a year's time. Mentally he was still as sharp as when he ran number rackets during the mid 1930's with Harlem's legend Bumpy Johnson or when he controlled a heroin ring in the 50's and 60's, but physically he knew he was nearing the end. His life as a gangster had allowed him to retire from the streets to a nice size home he had purchased upstate, in the city of Peekskill. Sadly, he hadn't been able to enjoy the beautiful home for quite some time. He was confined to his bedroom, which had been transformed into his own private care facility. Stubborn as a bull, he refused to spend his last days in a sterile white room in Peekskill Hospital or at Westledge nursing home waiting to die, choosing the familiar comfort of his own home instead. Rarely did anyone come to visit anymore, it seemed the closer he got to death the more people behaved like he was in the ground already. Death isn't contagious but that's how he was treated. With most of his family still living in New York City and either unwilling or unable to make the journey upstate to check on him, he spent most of his time surrounded by home care attendants. But there was one person who hadn't forgotten about him and came to visit faithfully, his grandson Hassan, his only daughter's only son. The similarities between the two were obvious to anyone who saw them. Hassan took after his grandfather in every way, mirroring the elder's quiet demeanor and studying his mannerisms. Even their looks were identical; smooth, dark brown skin, an engaging smile and pale green eyes. Hassan's slender frame hadn't filled out yet but staring at his grandson was like looking at himself as a teenager.

Hassan entered the room and nodded his head at the home attendant seated in the corner, entertaining herself with a crossword puzzle. She nodded back and smiled before getting up to exit the room, giving the two of them some privacy.

"Just yell if ya need me fa anyting'," she said in her thick Jamaican accent.

"Ok," Hassan replied offering a slight smile in return as he pulled a chair up next to the bed and had a seat.

Seeing his grandfather in his condition cut deep into Hassan as he tried his best to keep the tears forming in his eyes from falling. His grandfather was the closest thing he ever had to a father. The family's good name was built on his blood, sweat and gun work. His reputation was well known and still respected in the streets of Harlem. He had spent long stretches of his life in Elmira and Dannemora Prison, amongst the most hardened criminals and none of that had broken him. But the thing that defined him for so many years was rapidly quitting on him, his heart. It had been filled with so much love for those he cared for and not an ounce of fear of those he considered his adversaries. His biggest strength was now his greatest weakness. Hassan didn't like the powerless feeling he felt staring at the man who meant so much to him. His emotions teetered between sadness and anger at the realization that he couldn't prevent God's will for taking its natural course. After staring for a few more minutes and wiping away a couple tears that had managed to escape, a smile crept across his face seeing his grandfather's eyes slowly open and focus on him.

"Hey Pop-Pop, how you feeling?" Hassan asked, the genuine concern in his voice evident.

"Never felt better," the old man answered in a hoarse whisper. "Didn't expect to see you again so soon. That can't be good," he said between taking in breaths of air through the oxygen tubes in his nose.

"My fault, I thought I could come see you as much as I wanted," Hassan threw both his hands up in surrender and laughed.

"Anytime," his grandfather concurred. "It would be nice to see Monica walk through that door one of these days."

The mention of his mother caught Hassan off guard. For as long as he could remember his grandfather hadn't spoken to or of her. It was like she didn't exist to him anymore. The shame she caused him was too much to bear. The tracks on her arms told the story of the many bad choices she had made in life. She had fallen in love with the most dangerous boy on the block, who went by many names; Sugar Hill, Black Rain, China White or simply Heroin. The drug made slaves out its users and had long severed Hassan's mother and grandfather's once unbreakable bond. Her lust for a fix caused her to ache and itch and she fell into the clutches of a slick mouthed pimp, who fed her addiction in order to control her mind and body. Hearing his grandfather speak about her, let him know the end was near for the old man and he was trying to right all of his wrongs before it was too late. But the cold war between the two may have made things irreparable.

"My mother?" Hassan asked still unsure he had heard him right. "I haven't seen her in weeks and wouldn't know where to begin to look for her," he said lowering his head. He felt a similar shame at what she had become. Her choice of lifestyle had forced his hand as well and he had chosen the other side of the drug game— dealing. Hassan had stopped attending school after accepting a job with El Jefe and was making good money selling coke for him at least he thought so.

"I see that look in your eyes when your mother's name is brought up. You can't hide the shame on your face," his grandfather said. "You are more like her than you know tho. You should be ashamed of yourself, not her," he scolded.

Hassan shifted in his seat not liking or understanding where his grandfather was coming from. *I'm nothing like my mother,* he thought to himself. She was weak, she knew the trappings of the street, she had been raised around the dope game her whole life. She witnessed firsthand what the drug her father made his living selling did to people and still she had fallen victim to it. *Nah he wasn't like her at all,* he told himself, they were total opposites. If anything he was just like the man lying in the bed in front of him.

"I'm not like her at all Pop. I'm like you, I'm cut from your cloth," Hassan said proudly, almost boasting as he beamed with a sense of pride.

"Nah, you not like me son," he said solemnly. "You not like me at all. What you think because you push a little dope it makes us alike? Hmm? What, 'cause you got a little cash in your pockets, it makes you a man? A man stands on his own two feet," he informed his grandson. Even on his death bed he was giving Hassan the game, whether the young blood knew it or not. "Tell me something, why you think I'm ashamed of your mother?" he quizzed the youngster.

"Because she sells her body and shoot her profit in her arms. She a junkie and a whore," Hassan said the disdain he felt for her dripping off of every word. His green eyes darkened with hate.

"That's what you think?" he spoke between hacking coughs as he sat up in the bed. He took in a deep breath of air through the tubes in his nose before continuing, "I'm ashamed of her because I raised her to be a boss not a worker. If she was gonna hoe, I'd rather she did it for herself, not some jive motherfucker thinking he Goldie the Mack. Selling herself and dropping her bankroll off to him is why I'm ashamed. You ain't no different, selling the next man's dope and dropping your bankroll off to him at the end of the night. You a hoe too, just without the dirt on your knees," he spoke the harsh truth to his grandson. "You wanna impress me, you stand on your own two feet. You build your own empire. I don't care what it is you do. You wanna be a doctor, a professional ball player, a hustler, I don't give a shit Hassan. You just better be the best at it. You wanna sell dope, then you be the best dope dealer these streets ever seen, you hear me?"

Hassan stared in shock, he had never expected to be having this talk with his grandfather. But everything his Pop-Pop was saying made perfect sense to him. If he was going to be in the game, he needed to be playing to win.

"You hear me Hassan?" the old man repeated, hoping his words were reaching home and the young man was soaking up the game he was giving him. He always gave his grandson the truth but never this raw. But he refused to waste an opportunity to give Hassan some vital keys to life, after all he never knew when it could be his last chance to do so.

"Yeah I hear you Pop. I understand," Hassan declared.

"Good. Let me tell you something and I want you remember this. No man is better than the next man. The one who succeeds is the man who works the hardest and the smartest."

Hassan let the words sink into his brain as he sat silent. Sadly this would be the last lesson he would receive from his sickly fatherly figure but it had served its purpose. The hustler spirit in him had been awaken. The love for the game was in his blood. It was a part of his lineage. Soon the streets would know and his name would ring like church bells on Sunday.

CHAPTER FOUR

1986

The crack epidemic had hit the streets of New York like a tidal wave. Bringing with it more money than the streets had ever seen, making young niggas like Hassan rich, seemingly overnight. But with more money came more violence as rival crews shot it out over prime real estate turning neighborhoods into the Wild West. The Bronx seemed to be the epicenter of it all. Placing Hassan in the perfect position to profit, with a solid crew and a steady flow of coke from El

Jefe, he took over the Northside of Edenwald and its surrounding blocks with his signature green top crack vials. Hassan seemed to be opening up or taking over a new spot every week. If you wasn't buying from him or selling his product you couldn't get money on his side of the projects and he wouldn't hesitate to let his gun smoke to prove his point. Hassan stayed strapped and so did every member of his crew, a must in Edenwald where it was known that the two sides of the projects didn't get along.

The Southside was ran by an OG named Dopeman Dave, who didn't particular care for Hassan's young and brash ways. But Hassan didn't give a fuck, he was making money and enjoyed showing it off. El Jefe's love for expensive cars had rubbed off on him, after years of going to car shows with him. It was nothing to see Hassan and his crew pulling up on the block in the new Benz's, Beamers and Porsches. It became a guessing game to see what they would pull up in next, trying to see who could out shine the other. Dave was more old school in his approach and felt Hassan should be paying homage to his OG status. Instead he had Southside hustlers secretly buying from him along with hustlers from neighboring projects and crack heads from Dave's side of the projects coming north to cop their drugs. The OG's building resentment had tensions high throughout the projects.

"The pussy is freeeeee, but the crack cost moneyyyy, oh yeah," Twin sang along with the song blasting out the system in Hassan's 190 Benz as they cruised up Baychester and turned on Boston Road.

"Yo we need to hit Fordham. It's a nice day, you know the freaks is out," Hassan said as he turned down the music.

"No doubt B," Twin replied. "I'm wit it."

"You strapped?" Hassan asked.

"Ain't I always," Twin quickly answered.

"Just making sure nigga," he said. Hassan felt his beeper vibrating and snatched it off his hip to check the number. "Yo I need to find a pay phone. This dem niggas from Secor I told you about. This is about some money," he said switching lanes and weaving in between traffic causing Twin to have to hold on. Hassan was known for his crazy driving.

"Damn nigga," Twin barked causing Hassan to laugh.

"You scared nigga, get a dog," he replied.

The two pulled into the gas station and stopped in front of the two pay phones. Hassan jumped out in a haste, leaving his door open behind him. He was dressed in a custom made Dapper Dan short set with two big gold rope chains that bounced off his chest as he walked. Lifting the phone off the jack and placing it between his ear and his shoulder, Hassan looked down at the beeper and began to dial the number.

The sound of tires screeching through the parking lot made him look up from his beeper. He saw a dark face with shades aiming an Uzi at him just before he heard the thunderous sound of gunfire. He had been set up. Hassan ducked for cover, barely escaping the bullets hitting the phone over his head, where he had just been standing. He crawled back to the car, climbing into the driver seat as the windows in the car began to shatter from being hit with bullets. Glass was everywhere, Twin reached for his gun out of what used to be the window trying to return fire but was struck in the hand by a bullet causing him to drop his gun inside the car. Hassan managed to throw the car in reverse and weaved his way out the gas station and onto the street. He threw it in drive and sped off down the block escaping the attempt on his life.

"Oh shit, these niggas tried to body us," he said as he continued navigating through traffic, trying to get as far away from the scene as possible. He removed his gun from his stash spot and placed it on his lap. He was absolutely sure the hit had been ordered by Dopeman Dave, the shooter in the dark glasses was a known henchmen of his. Hassan was already plotting his retaliation. "That nigga Dave is dead B. That nigga body gon' drop before the weekend is over. And I'm getting at dem ma'fuckas from Secor too, you feel me?" he said but received no answer. Hassan looked over at Twin who laid slumped and lifeless against the door, his eyes wide open.

"Twin...Twin," he called out to him while shaking his body but there was still no response. It was then he saw the hole in Twin's head and all the blood running down the side of his face against the door. He knew Twin was gone but still drove straight to the hospital.

Hassan sat in a chair consumed by his thoughts, massaging his temples as he watched Twin's identical brother, Birdie, pace back and forth in the living room, while he grieved silently. The whole crew filled the apartment in Mount Vernon to mourn and discuss how they were going to retaliate against Dopeman Dave's crew. There had been constant tension between the two factions but it was now an all-out war. Hassan felt responsible for Twin's death, those bullets were meant for him and he wouldn't rest easy until Dave's blood ran in the streets.

"Yo, I gotta kill this nigga myself," Birdie shouted. "If anybody else do it, it ain't right. It don't mean shit. He killed my twin," he said to Hassan with tears in his eyes and a 40 oz. in his hand.

Hassan definitely understood where Birdie was coming from as he heard the hurt and anger in his voice. He too was seeing red, Dave had tried him. Everybody in the room knew who the hit was meant for and so did the streets. Twin had just been caught in the crossfire. Still in all, somebody had to die, an eye for an eye, the streets were waiting to see how he reacted. They all knew the rules of war but Hassan was a master at seeing more and although he knew Birdie wouldn't like it, he couldn't let him be the one to avenge his brother's death. Hassan had a plan and it would kill two birds with one stone. Now that they were in a war, there was much to be gained from killing Dave but it had to be done right.

"Yo I got an idea," Hassan spoke up, lifting his head from a deep thought. "I got a way for us to knock Dopeman Dave out the box and take over the whole projects," he said. "But you won't be the one to pull the trigger B," he said looking over at Birdie. "I need you to be cool with that, if not we can do it your way. I'm fucked up behind this shit too, we all are. You know I had nothing but love for Twin but I know that nobody is feeling it like you. So if it makes you feel better to be the one that kills Dave, fuck it that's what it will be. But if we do it my way, we'll not only kill but conquer. Either way it's your call."

Birdie looked around the room into each member of the crew's eyes, then looked at Hassan and said, "What's your plan?"

"Nigga hurry up," Frog screamed as he grew impatient watching Vel recount his money for the third time. "You make this shit take way longer than it has to," he said.

"I need my count to be right, I ain't with the bullshit. If I'm off by a dollar I'm recounting," Vel shot back.

"Either the count is right or it ain't, ain't no more to it. Ain't no money reappearing or disappearing, it's just me, you and this nigga in here," he said nodding in the direction of the goon leaned against the wall. Dopeman Dave had keeping an eye on them as they counted his money.

Frog and Vel ran two of Dave's most profitable

spots in the projects, slanging red and orange tops respectively. Dave made sure all his spots sold different color vials, so he could keep track of who was moving more crack. He looked at it as a friendly competition, an incentive for his workers to hustle harder. Dopeman Dave had run his operation the same way for years even back when he sold heroin. He had been in business all these years and had never seen the inside of a jail cell. Some said it was luck, others said it was because of his duplicity, serving up other dealers in order to stay in business. Either way Dave had made a bunch of money and had the means to go to war with the Northside crew.

He was a different type of boss from Hassan. Rarely was he seen in the streets. Dave never got his hands dirty when it came to anything, drugs or murder. He much rather sit back, count money and give orders. He would always say, "If I had to move all the drugs and kill all the niggas myself, you muthafuckas would never make no money. Call it job security." He put ten thousand on Hassan's head and sat back waiting for his body to drop. For him that was a drop in a bucket.

"Pass me that bag," Vel yelled.

Frog was happy as hell seeing Vel starting to put

the dough in the duffle bag. They had been at it for half the night. "Good, call that nigga Dave and tell him we ready," he said looking over to the henchmen.

Dave's henchmen slowly pulled the car into the dark alley and flashed his lights. He waited until a set of headlights flashed back at him before he proceeded. Driving a little further into the alley, he pulled alongside a parked Lincoln and came to a stop. Vel sat in the passenger seat while Frog sat in the back. This was the routine they followed every time they made a drop off to Dave. He was old school. He insisted on being the one to pick up his own money. He didn't need any middle men skimming off the top.

Looking in the adjacent vehicle, they saw Dopeman Dave with his signature Cazals and fur trimmed coat on, in the backseat twirling a toothpick in his mouth. Like usual, his driver and main henchmen sat in the front seat with their guns fully exposed in their shoulder holsters ready for whatever.

"Hurry the fuck up, ain't nobody got all night," Dave's big voice boomed from the backseat. He was clearly upset at having to wait on them. "And it better not be short, as long as I been out here waiting on you two motherfuckers."

"Our shit ain't never short Dave, you know that,"

Frog declared.

"Yeah, well good thing you can count, cause you sure nuff can't tell time," Dave said causing the two men in the front seat to laugh.

"Pop the trunk," Vel said to the henchmen in the car with him then hopped out. Walking to the back of the car, he snatched both bags out the trunk and put them over his shoulder. He walked to the back of Dave's car and dropped both bags in the trunk that was already open then slammed it shut. "It's all good," he said tapping the trunk after closing it.

"What was the count?" Dave asked.

"55,000 on the dot," Frog shouted from the backseat.

"Ok," Dave said seemingly satisfied.

No one in the car noticed that Vel had walked back from behind their vehicle holding a semiautomatic weapon in his hand. The darkness of the alley allowed him to conceal it with ease. Without warning Frog shot Dave's henchmen that had drove them in the back of the head from the backseat and then Vel opened fire on Dave's car, killing the two men in the front first. Then turning his gun on Dopeman Dave as he tried to exit, hitting him in the back and chest. Dave stumbled down the alley trying to escape as Vel gave chase, hitting him a few more times with shots. Dave finally collapsed to the ground when one of the bullets hit him in the back of the head. When the shooting stopped, Frog pulled the dead driver out the front seat of the car they rode in, while Vel reached into Dave's car popping the trunk once again and removed the two duffle bags filled with cash. Their reward for the hit, courtesy of Hassan who had used Dave's own money to get him killed.

The fleet of BMW's, Audi's and Mercedes' pulling up in front of the building on the Southside, made the parking lot look like a car show. But this wasn't about putting on for the hood, it was strictly business. Hassan hopped out of his Benz, his fade freshly cut, dressed in jeans and a leather bomber, a crisp pair of timberlands and his gold chain with a large anchor medallion on full display. He was flanked by members of his crew, all freshly dressed and armed with guns in hand, as he approached the group of men sitting on a few benches.

"What y'all niggas doing out here?" Hassan asked smoothly. "Who y'all pumping for?" he continued in a calm tone but became more aggressive when no one responded. "C'mon don't everybody answer at once.

Who y'all pumping for?" he asked clapping his hands in front of him as he spoke.

"Dave," one of the men announced.

"Dave is dead, so who y'all pumping for?" Hassan asked once again. "If you not selling green tops you can't get money in Edenwald no more," he barked. "Ain't no freelancing, from here on out it's my way. You either roll or get rolled over, ya feel me."

Hassan and his crew had been running up on dealers from the Southside all week letting everybody know what the new rules in the projects were. Most niggas fell in line, after all Hassan was offering a better product at a cheaper price with the chance to make more money. He was showing love. Niggas started filling their gates with his work almost immediately, essentially turning their spots into his. Those that didn't and tried to grip up against him were quickly squashed. Unlike Dave, Hassan didn't mind doing his own dirty work. He was always on the front line, out front and center, banging his hammer.

"This how it go, every spot keep 20 percent of the profits, spot manager is responsible for paying the lookouts, runners and pitchers out of his share. If y'all wit dat, my nigga Frog will spin the block, drop off that package and we can start making this money. If not y'all know what it is," Hassan said then turned and walked back to his car not waiting for them to answer.

CHAPTER FIVE

RHAE

Rhae sat in her car staring at the massive building for over 15 minutes before she found the strength to get out and make her way inside. Her heart was racing once again and she felt flushed with all types of emotions as she sat at the table waiting to see the man she considered her mentor. Almost 8 years had passed since he had last laid eyes on her and her on him. Rhae tapped her foot and bounced her legs allowing her nerves to get the best of her. She wondered what he looked like and how he was holding up. She hoped he thought she had grown into a beautiful young lady. His opinion of her mattered more than anyone she could think of. Shank had been the closest thing to a fatherly figure she ever had and gave her the closest thing to a family she had ever known. So she knew her visit was long overdue. Although she had kept in contact with him through mail, this was her very first visit to the jail and the waiting was killing her. She thought back to the first time she met him and a smile eased across her face. He was truly one of a kind.

1978

The thunderous sound of the front door busting open was immediately followed by the loud, fear-filled shrieks of the young girl being dragged across the floor of the shooting gallery.

"No!" Charlene cried out, the fear she felt quickly racing through her veins, flooding her heart. Her pleas for help fell on deaf ears. A room filled with dope fiends wasn't a place to look for sympathy.

The burned out abandoned apartments served as a spot where addicts could cop and shoot heroin. The drug made zombies out of its users, who were scattered all over the apartment in various stages. A brown skinned woman, who had long been robbed of her looks, sat at a table with a belt around her arm, gripping the other end between her teeth as she prepared to propel herself into nirvana. While others nodded off with syringes at their sides or dangling from their arms already caught in the deadly drugs rapture.

"Let her go!" Rhae screamed as she kicked and flailed her body trying to free herself from the grasp of the two young goons holding her by the arms as they entered the apartment.

"Shut that lil' bitch up," the leader of the group of dealers named Fats said as he strolled in behind the rest of the group. "Take them in the back," he instructed. Fats had an axe to grind with the two girls. They had schemed him out of some bank weeks earlier that led to him receiving a beating from his boss. The blackish purple circle that remained around his eye reminding him on a daily.

Charlene and Rhae were sisters of circumstance, two kindred spirits, runaways force to survive the best way they knew how on the streets. Boosting out of department stores, pickpocketing, scheming and scamming, they were pros at all of them. Seventeen year old Charlene was the leader, 2 years older than Rhae, she looked out for her on the streets, teaching the young girl the ropes. Their hustle determined how much they ate at night or if they did at all. Charlene *was beautiful and she knew it, using her looks to bait in unsuspecting victims. She knew most men thought with the head in their pants and she used that to her advantage. She had done the same with Fats and had hit the jackpot. But she had gotten greedy and went against her own rule in search of another big score. The two girls never hit the same side of town so close together but Charlene couldn't help going back to the well once more. Rhae was against it but allowed the older Charlene to talk her into doing it. But while they thought they were running game on another unsuspecting hustler, they were the ones being set up. One of the boys recognized her and sent word to Fats, who lured them to a spot in the projects and delivered a beating of his own to the two girls. Sparing the young Rhae a bit, he saved most of his rage for Charlene, leaving her bruised and battered but he wasn't done.*

"C'mon," he waved as the group followed him down the hall. He kicked open the door to one of the backrooms, startling the occupants, then pulling his gun from his waist, waving it at the dope fiends in the room. "Get outta here, muthafuckas," he barked. They quickly cleared out not wanting to upset one of the gatekeepers to their medicine. "Toss that bitch on the bed," he yelled pointing to the dirty mattress on the floor in the middle of the room, where two dope fiends had just been laying fucking one another.

Charlene curled up in a ball as she was slammed down on the mattress, sobbing uncontrollably. She had never been in this much danger. Dodging policemen and department store security came easy to her, but this was different. Fats and his goons were ruthless, she had crossed the wrong individuals and now they were in too deep.

"You took from me bitch, now it's my turn," Fats said staring down at her as he unbuckled the belt holding up his slacks. "You gon' pay me what you owe and you gon' pay in pussy. To me and the fellas," he said dropping down on his knees on the mattress as he began tugging at Charlene's bell bottomed jeans and tearing her blouse exposing her white bra.

"Get off of her!" Rhae screamed continuing to try to free herself but the boys were twice her size and strength and it was to no avail.

Charlene wasn't about to let Fats violate her and fought with everything in her to keep him from doing just that. Fats reached his hand up to the sky and came down hard and fast across her face splitting her lip, causing her to see stars, knocking all the fight out of her in one swift, powerful strike.

"Be still bitch," he said pulling her bra down revealing her breast. The sight made his dick harden instantly. Fats had been dying to fuck her. It was why he let his guard down, falling victim to her the first time. But he was about to get some payback and she was now the victim.

"Get off of her you fucking pervert," Rhae spat. "You black piece of shit!" she yelled.

"I thought I told one of you to shut that lil bitch up," Fats said looking back over his shoulder than standing back up. "I think you the one who needs the lesson," he said stalking over to her. He grabbed her little face squeezing it in his hand until she looked like a fish. "I'm gonna teach you bitches a lesson you'll never forget," he said removing a bag of dope from his pocket, holding it up in front of his face and plucking it. "Bring back one of them junkies," he instructed. "I'ma tighten you up real nice, ya dig."

"So this what y'all do when I'm not around," a deep baritone voice came spilling into the room grabbing everyone's attention.

Shank stood in the doorway dressed in a short, brown, leather trench coat with the collar slightly flipped up, a beige turtle neck sweater, a pair of slacks and shoes. Tall, dark and handsome with a neatly groomed afro and mustache, Shank looked like money, "The Smack Man" as he was called. Shank was one of the biggest fish in a big pond. Only 25 years old, he controlled most of the heroin in the Bronx but his organization operated out of Soundview projects, using various apartments to package, store and sell his product that he called "Messiah." Fiends came from all over to get a taste of his brand of dope, which had its share of deaths attached to it. That only added to the allure.

"Nah Shank, we was just jiving, having a little fun that's all," Fats said seeing his boss standing in the doorway.

Shank strolled into the room kicking an empty bottle of cheap wine out of his path as he made his way over to Charlene. He squatted down next to her as she laid on the mattress and turned her face, so that he could look at her. "Don't look like these young ladies are having that much fun," he said examining her bruises. "Only a weak cat forces himself on a fox," he said standing up and putting his hand out to help Charlene to her feet as she fixed herself. "I apologize to you ladies," he said smoothly.

"It's not your fault, it's that muthafucka right there," she said holding her blouse together with one hand while lunging at Fats only to be stopped by Shank.

"Calm down," he said smoothly trying to put out the flames shooting from her eyes towards her attacker. "The responsibility always falls on the person in charge," he informed her.

"And that's you?" she asked but clearly knew the answer. She would have to be blind and stupid not to recognize his power.

Shank just smiled and chuckled slightly.

"Shank man, these the bitches that stole the money from me," Fats said.

"Oh yeah," he replied. "These two," he asked rhetorically. "You two took something that belonged to me. Didn't your parents teach you not to steal?" he questioned.

"We ain't got no parents," Rhae responded full of attitude.

"No parents?" Shank questioned. "What y'all some orphans?"

"Runaways," Rhae corrected him. "And with all due respect we needed that money to eat," Rhae said unapologetically.

"Let her go," he instructed the boys holding her arms. "I like you Lil' Bit," he said with a smile giving her a nickname. She was bold, though small in stature he could tell she had a lot of heart. She spoke to him with more confidence than most grown men in the streets. "Fats, I think you owe Lil Bit here and her friend an apology."

"Sister," Rhae corrected him again. "Charlene is my sister."

"Ok," Shank said.

"Lil' Bit and her sister."

"Sorry," Fats said clearly not meaning it but knowing better than to object an order from Shank.

"Have you two ladies eaten today?" he asked.

"No," Rhae said.

"But we are ok, we just want to leave," Charlene quickly interjected.

"It's the least I can do," Shank said but truth was he wanted to keep the young ladies in his presence a little while longer before he let them walk free. He needed to feel them out to see if they would run to the cops. That was something he definitely didn't need, he drew enough heat on his own and wouldn't hesitate to bury the two young girls if he felt the need to. "Please let me put some food in your stomachs and maybe some money in your pockets," he said knowing it would spark their interest.

"Ok," they both finally agreed.

Shank pulled his black deuce and a quarter into the driveway of the beautiful home on the outskirts of the city and cut off the engine. The two girls' heads swiveled as they took in the immaculate neighborhood in amazement. New Rochelle was only a few minutes outside the city but it was worlds away from anything either of them had ever witnessed. Shank had a slight grin on his face as he looked in his rearview mirror at the look on Rhae's face. She hadn't been totally hardened by the streets yet, the way he and Charlene had, and her face lit up like it was Christmas day looking at the homes that surrounded her.

"Whose house is this?" Charlene quickly asked. Though she admired the neighborhood she wasn't about to let her guard down. She didn't know Shank from a can of paint and she had seen too much living out on the street to fully trust anybody. "What are we doing here? You said you were taking us to eat. What's going on?" she asked almost concurrently she was speaking so fast.

"Cool your jets, mama. This is my pad. Everything is on the up and up," he said putting his hand on her thigh sending jolt up her spine and a tingle through her panties. "I figured a fox like you wouldn't want to be seen out in a restaurant in your condition," he said smoothly, pointing towards her ripped blouse, then flipping the visor down on her side so she could see her swollen lip in the mirror. "I figured I could practice my cooking skills on you two. Plus I have some clothes in the house that belonged to an ex lady friend of mine I think you could fit."

"No slick shit," Charlene warned him pointing her finger at him.

"You either," he replied. "Y'all the thieves remember," he joked then exited the car.

Shank entered the house with the two girls following close behind. His house was decked out, an all beige sofa and love seat with leather upholstery positioned nicely around a mink rug stretched across the floor nicely decorated living room. A large floor model TV sat against the wall surrounded by the most elaborate stereo system either of the girls had ever seen. His home looked like a man of his stature lived there.

"Make yourselves at home," he said removing his coat and laying it across the back of the sofa. "The clothes are in the closet in the first room on your left," he said as he pointed Charlene towards the steps. "Anything you like you can have."

Charlene looked over at Rhae unsure if leaving her alone with Shank was a good idea. She was truly the overprotective sister Rhae never had.

"She'll be ok," Shank said seeing the look on her face, trying to put those fears to rest. Neither of the girls knew it but they were safer than they had ever been in the past few hours. Shank had no plans on harming either one of them and while in his presence no one would dare do a thing to them.

"I'm fine," Rhae reassured allowing Charlene to finally ascend the steps.

"Have a seat Lil' Bit," Shank invited. "You want a soda?" he offered.

"Yeah," she said.

Shank disappeared into the kitchen but not before Rhae noticed the gun in the small of his back. She knew he was a *gangster but for some reason he didn't scare her but she also remained on point already mapping her escape plan in her head if things went left. Rhae was extremely smart for her age. She adapted to street life quickly, picking up every trick to the trade Charlene showed her and a few she learned on her own. Stick boney but she was much tougher than her baby face would lead anyone to believe and although she played the little sister role to Charlene, she was a leader at heart and no one's sidekick.*

"Here you go," Shank said returning with her soda. "I'm gonna start dinner, cuz I don't know about you but I'm starvin' like Marvin."

Rhae smiled, "Me too."

Shank and Charlene sat at the table finishing up their plates, but they both seemed to be more interested in talking than eating. Rhae had long finished and was in the living room watching TV, leaving the two of them alone. Shank was interested in Charlene's story, trying to find out where she had been in life and what led to her being on the streets. Her story was not too far off from his and he found himself intrigued by her. He listened more than he talked, getting an understanding for the hopeless, empty look he saw in her eyes. Her beauty was undeniable and he knew her pain well but as the hours past and her wall slowly came down, he got a glimpse at the real her.

"I got the dishes," Charlene said as she stood to her feet and began collecting their plates.

"You don't have to..." he started but was quickly interrupted.

"It's the least I can do," she said. "The food was great by the way. Where'd you learn to cook like that?"

"Can't tell you all my secrets," he said as he followed her into the kitchen, leaning up against the doorway. He watched her maneuver in his kitchen, washing, drying and putting away dishes making herself right at home. It had been a while since he'd seen a woman in his kitchen and he had to admit he liked it. "You know y'all are more than welcome to stay, I can take you where y'all need to go in the morning if you want," he offered. "I have plenty room, no strings," he said crossing his heart then smiling.

Damn there goes that smile again, she thought to herself. She quickly was falling for his smooth boss ways and million dollar grin. She knew a man like him had his pick when it came to women, it came with the game and came with the power. She was attracted to the same things about him. Charlene was far from naïve but she didn't care about those other women, she wanted to be the main woman in his life. "I don't know if that's a good idea," she said even though everything in her wanted to say yes, she didn't want to look over zealous.

"Ok," he said.

Her heart sunk in her chest. She hoped he would try convincing her but he hadn't. Charlene had missed her shot and she instantly regretted it.

"I'm gonna go check on Lil' Bit," he said disappearing from the doorway even before the words left his lips.

"Fuck," she silently mouthed to herself. "Why did you say no?" she continued talking to herself.

"I think you might have to reconsider," Shank said startling her.

Charlene turned to see him standing in the doorway once again but now he was holding a sleeping Rhae in his arms. She felt butterflies in her stomach, seeing Rhae in his arms made her feel like they were a family, something she hadn't had in a longtime, so for a moment she let herself believe that they were. "I think you're right," she said. Inside she was happy to have a second chance to say yes.

Shank headed up the steps and laid Rhae on the bed in one of his spare rooms and covered her with a blanket. He hit the light and headed back downstairs. Returning to the kitchen he found it empty. But heard Charlene call his name from the living room. He opened the freezer and grabbed some ice placing it inside of a towel and joined her in the living room. As he reached the entrance the sensual sound of Teddy Pendergrass' "Close the Door" filled the room.

Charlene stood in front of his stereo system moving her body slowly and sexily to the music. She seemed to be lost in the groove as Shank admired her from the back. Her slim but curvy body figure moving effortlessly. He was captured by the sway of her hips and wanted nothing more than to creep up behind her and join in but he played it cool.

"Hmm Mm," he said clearing his throat letting her know he was standing there.

She turned to face him but didn't stop dancing. "This is my cut. You have all the jams," she said admiring his vast music collection.

He walked towards her and she put her arms on his shoulder and snaked her body from side to side trying to entice him to dance with her but Shank wasn't the dancing type.

"Here this should help your lips," he said lifting the towel with ice up eye level, while trying to remain even kilt.

"So should this," Charlene said before leaning in and kissing him only to have him pull back from her. She was immediately embarrassed and turned to get away.

Shank grabbed her waist and pulled her back to him, he could feel the weight in her body shift as she felt his rejection. "Where you going?" he asked.

She just looked down at the ground not answering him.

Shank lifted her head up so she was looking him in the

eye. "You don't owe me anything," he said sincerely. "You don't have to do anything you don't want to," he said needing to make it clear to her that what he had done for them was out of the kindness of his heart and not for no other reason.

"I know," she said. "And I know what I want."

Shank leaned in and kissed her, slipping his tongue into her mouth. Their tongues waltzed with each other as Shank began to remove her clothes and she did the same to his. He lifted her up off her feet carrying her over to the couch and placing her down gently. Shank kneeled between her legs and removed her jeans and panties effortlessly. Charlene spread her legs as he dived mouth first and tasted her, licking and sucking up all her juices. Shank was more experienced than any man she had ever been with and his tongue took her body to places she had never been before. She moaned and squirmed from the amount of pleasure she was receiving and soon she felt a rush come over her body she had never felt before as her legs began to tremble uncontrollably.

Charlene screamed in pure bliss as she reached an orgasmic state for the first time in her life. Shank dropped his slacks and stroked his rock hard manhood, preparing to enter her sweet spot. Charlene spread her legs wide inviting him in but was forced to hold her breath as she felt his girth *enter her walls. Shank slowly stroked her allowing Charlene the chance to get used to his size, her wetness allowing him to glide in and out as she moaned. Charlene grinded and pumped her hips back and forth taking every thrust and wanted more. Shank picked up the pace, giving her hard and deep strokes as she called out his name. He quickly flipped her over bending her over the couch, her body had a slight glisten as it sweated from the workout she was receiving. Shank entered her from behind and continued delivering long, deep strokes until it felt like he was swimming in a pool of her love juices. Charlene moans increased as she felt his pole begin to pulsate as he approached his climax. Finally, Shank let out a roar as he pulled out of her, ejaculating on her butt. Charlene didn't move she felt tingles shooting all through her body. Shank was definitely the best sex partner she had ever had and she couldn't get enough and it wasn't long before they were at it again. The two sexed deep into the middle of the night.*

Rhae sat at the kitchen table counting large stacks of cash, placing rubber bands on each one, than writing down the tally in the notebook next to her. The last year seemed to have sped by, Shank had taken them in and the three of them had become like a family. He had also expanded his empire while switching his hustle. He now controlled all the

coke in the city and was making more money than he ever had.

While Shank's relationship with Charlene was of the romantic nature, he sported her on his arm at the hottest spots in New York while keeping her in nothing but the finest clothes by the top designers. His relationship with Rhae was more of a mentor or big brother type. She was his protégé and he taught her everything he knew about the drug game, showing her how to weigh, cut and bag up coke. Rhae was the perfect student, she was a quick study and had gotten to the point where she could eyeball weight. She kept his books and knew which of his spots were making what and knew when a crew of his was coming up short. She truly was his second pair of eyes on his lucrative business.

"You still up counting that money," Charlene said as she entered the kitchen dressed in a red silk robe. She floated through the kitchen like the queen of the house. She was definitely enjoying her seat on the throne next to the king of the city.

"Yup," Rhae said as she slapped Charlene's hand away from the money. "Gots to be right," she said. Her love for making and counting money was only matched by Shank himself.

"Sho ya right, Lil Bit," Shank said strolling in to the kitchen fully dressed prepared to start his day. "Some people, gotta have it," he crooned.

"Some people, really need it," Rhae joined in.

"Do thangs, do thangs, bad thangs...for the love of moneyyyy," they sung in unison before sharing a laugh.

Charlene just sucked her teeth and exited the kitchen.

"What's her problem," Rhae asked.

"What's not her problem," Shank said shaking his head.

"The count is right," Rhae said as she wrote the final number in the notebook. "I counted it twice.

"Your word is good enough for me," Shank said as he picked up the money and started placing it in a large leather bag.

The sound of the front door crashing in caught them all by surprise. In an instant, life as they knew it had been interrupted as police flooded the house with guns drawn. Shank had nowhere to run and was caught red handed with tons of illegal tender stacked up on the kitchen table.

Charlene's cries could be heard throughout the neighborhood as she stood in front of the house in her robe watching as they led a handcuffed Shank out of the house and placed him in a waiting patrol car. Someone had dropped a dime on Shank, it was the only way they could knock him of his throne. He stared at his two girls through the window from the backseat and forced a smile, hoping it would ease their pain. Charlene was hysterical and probably didn't even notice the look on his face but Rhae saw it and smiled back at him as he nodded back at her just as the squad car pulled off.

Rhae walked in to the street and watched as the car pulled out of the neighborhood, she stared until the blue and white cars disappeared. She was so focused in on Shank, she hadn't noticed the middle aged white lady in the business suit and clipboard approaching her.

"Rhaenelle Price," the woman called out.

"Yeah," Rhae said turning around trying to figure out who the woman in front of her was and how she knew her name.

"I'm Sally English, I'm with social services. It has been brought to my office's attention that you are an underage runaway," she said. "I'm gonna need you to come with me. We will try to locate your parents and if that fails you will be turned over to the custody of the state," she stated coldly.

Before either Rhae or Charlene could protest officers grabbed Rhae and led her away to another waiting car. Charlene screamed for them to let her go but they ignored her. The officer pushed her out the way as he hopped in his car followed by Mrs. English and they drove off leaving Charlene sobbing as other officers tore the house apart.

Rhae sat in silence in the back of the car watching as the only sister she ever knew got further and further away.

Just like her mentor, Shank, she would be property of the state of New York for the next couple of years.

CHAPTER SIX

The sound of the big metal door opening caused Rhae to lift her head and snap out of her daydream. Shank strolled through the door with his signature smooth strut. He had aged some but he looked good for a man who had been in jail for the last decade. Gone was the afro he sported in the 70's replaced by a low cut fade. He was in even better shape than before and was still just as handsome. The small patch of grey in his goatee was the only evidence he had aged some. He nodded to the officer that had accompanied him and the man began removing his cuffs. Shank turned towards Rhae and winked causing her to cheese just like she did when she was younger. Sliding into the seat in front of her, he just stared for a moment, taking in the grown woman that sat across from him. Gone was the skinny little girl who was all knees and elbows, Rhae had blossomed into a stunning beauty. He was proud of her. She had survived something that most who were dealt her cards hadn't. He had instilled a lot of game and wisdom in her during their brief time together. He never wanted her to get caught up in the trappings of the street. Those corners ate young girls alive and he never wanted that for her. Inside he tried turning her into a female version of himself, full of game, full of knowhow and full of hustle. All the tools she would need to survive in a man's world.

"Lil Bit," he said joyously. "You finally got taller," he joked. "You are more beautiful than I could have imagined, even prettier than your pictures."

"Thank you," she said while blushing. "How you been?" she asked getting right to what she wanted to know. "They treating you good in here? How you holding up? You need anything? Have you been getting the money I been sending?" she rambled off.

"I'm doing good. You know I'm gonna be good wherever I'm at Lil' Bit. I got the guards in my pocket.

I eat good every night," he said leaning back rubbing his stomach. "And yes, I have been getting the money you send but I told you before I don't need it. Shit, do you need some money?" he teased showing her he was still sitting on a nice piece of cash from his days in the street.

Rhae just laughed it was good to hear him speaking like she remembered him. It showed that all the time spent behind bars hadn't broken his spirit.

"So when was the last time you spoke with Charlene?" he asked.

Rhae knew it was coming but she had no answer for him, she had long lost touch with her, just like he had. "It's been a while," she said. "And you?"

"Longer than that," he confessed. "She hasn't been to see me in about 6 years. I got a couple letters here and there but even that has stopped. It is what it is," he said. "It comes with the game. You win some you lose some."

Rhae just nodded her head. Charlene had cut the two people off who loved her the most but time had done its job and healing those scars Rhae felt and from the sound of it, it had done the same for Shank.

"So what's going on out in the streets, I'm hearing about this new shit called crack from all the young cats coming in here. I heard it got the streets like zombie land, people sucking on a glass pipe for a 10 minute high. I heard muthafuckas getting rich overnight out there," Shank said as Rhae could see the hustler in him come alive as he talked about the drug game.

"You know a lot for a person who been locked up so long," she joked.

"Knowledge is power," he replied with a smirk creeping across his face.

"So what's going on with your case? How's your appeal coming along?" she asked her voice full of concern.

"You want the truth or a lie," he asked.

"Of course I want the truth!"

"Well the truth is Rhae," he said calling her by her real name. "It don't look like I'll be getting out of here anytime soon or ever for that matter. The state had an air tight case, then they had a rat who I allowed to know too much and it came back to haunt me. Fats got on the stand and told them people everything, even made up a few things for good measure," he said shaking his head back and forth. "It's ok, I can sleep easy at night knowing I took my time like a man and ain't jam up nobody to save my own ass. You know a coward dies a thousand deaths."

It hurt her to hear him say he may never come home. Shank meant so much to her and she couldn't do anything to help him and he didn't want her to. He was fine doing his time. He just made her promise she wouldn't ever become a stranger like Charlene.

"I just want to personally thank you for everything you did for me as a young girl. You really saved my life and set me on a path that was different from where I was probably headed. I will always love you for that and forever be indebted to you," she said as tears dropped from her eyes.

"Stop all that crying," Shank said wiping her face. "We family Rhae you don't owe me anything, you understand that? Family," he said as he squeezed her hand and winked. "Family take care of each other."

Then the guard walked by and tapped the table signaling their visit was over. Shank stood to his feet and smiled once again. Then walked back through the big metal door he had emerged from.

CHAPTER SEVEN

HASSAN

Edenwald Houses had always been one of the most violent projects in the city. It was a war zone that bred gangsters but after Dopeman Dave's murder, Hassan had eased the tension by uniting the entire projects, making him a star not only in his hood but throughout the borough. He had elevated himself from a drug dealer to a street CEO and crack was his business. Hassan had spots not only in the projects but all over the Bronx, bringing in an average of about 350 thousand dollars a week. Under his leadership his crew was seeing a different type of money than most hustlers in the city and they stood out where ever they went. But Hassan stood out more than the rest. Full of charisma, charm, and blessed with good looks, he was liked by most who came in contact with him and that went double for females. Like any other man of his powerful status, he indulged in the spoils. He always kept company with some of the prettiest women in the city, redbones being his favorite and tonight was no different. He was returning from a trip to City Island after enjoying some seafood with a shorty he had met at the Rucker in Harlem. Hassan decided to cruise through Edenwald and check on his operation before heading to his low spot out in Mount Vernon with the light skinned shorty riding shotgun.

"I bet you take all your girls to City Island," shorty teased as she turned down the music some.

"Nah just the ugly ones, can't be seen in Manhattan with em," Hassan teased back.

"Oh so I'm ugly now, you foul," she said shaking her head.

"Nah, you know you got it going on," he said and he wasn't lying. "You wouldn't be riding wit me if you didn't."

"Is that right?" she questioned.

"Word," he said looking over at her lustfully.

The way he stared at her sent warm sensations through her panties, making her squirm in the leather seats of his car. He was definitely fine and getting money plus she had been secretly eyeballing the print in his jeans all night. Her horniness was building as she tried her best not to play herself out and do what came natural to her.

Hassan was well aware of her reputation as an oral Olympian, the streets talk and he had gotten a full report on her. His dick began to swell slightly in his pants as he stared at her nice full lips that were covered in red lipstick. The thought of her wrapping them around his manhood was driving him crazy but he played it smooth as usual.

"I'm feeling you," he said.

"Yeah?" she asked as she rubbed his leg then moved her hand to his dick, licking her lips as she felt his thick pole.

"Yeah," he repeated as she unbuttoned his pants, pulling his brick hard manhood out.

She gave it a few strokes with her hand before going down on him, taking him into her warm mouth while he drove through his projects. Hassan quickly understood why she had gained her reputation for having lethal lips as she polished his knob making it hard for him to drive straight. He palmed the back of her head guiding himself in and out of her mouth as he turned the corner on E.229th Street and pressed on the gas.

"Hold on, I need to stop and get something," he said pulling up in front of the store and stopping. He needed a reason to stop her, the shit was feeling too good and he didn't want to wrap his car around a telephone pole. "You want something out of here?" he asked.

"Some gum," she said as he hopped out and disappeared into the store.

As he exited the store, he saw a familiar face headed straight towards him. An old head who once was on top back in the day but had become another to join the ranks of the strung out crack addicts.

"Big time," the man chanted seeing the young hustler emerging from the store.

"What up old school," Hassan replied the man's name slipping his mind.

"Let me clean the windows on your ride," the man asked pulling a worn out spray bottle out of nowhere with some greenish blue liquid in it.

"Chill, chill," Hassan said stopping the man in his tracks. "I'm cool right now, but come check me tomorrow up at the car wash. I'll hook you up."

"Ok," the man smiled. "Well could you throw me a lil' somethin' somethin' now," he asked.

Hassan reached in his pocket and peeled off a few dollars and extended his hand towards the man who suddenly looked disappointed.

"I meant some of that other thang," he said doing a little two step dance.

Hassan shook his head. It hadn't been the first time the old head had hit him up for a freebie and he was sure it wouldn't be the last. Hassan remembered the man's run, he had always showed him love when he was younger. In turn Hassan still had nothing but respect for him even in his washed up state.

"Here," he said reaching in his coat and handing him one. "It's your lucky night."

"Thanks bigtime, I'm gonna be there tomorrow at the car wash waiting for you," the man said as he hurried off into the alley.

"You better be," Hassan said with a smile watching the man disappear down the alley. "Oh shit, I forgot the condoms," he said heading back into the store.

Fats had truly fallen all the way off. Once the man in the street, he was nothing but a bum and a fiend now. Most of the people he had told on were never coming home and most of the dealers running the streets now were too young to even know he had snitched. He scrambled around all day and night looking for ways to make a few dollars in order to get high. Hassan had just made his night giving him some crack to smoke. He raced down the alley and stepped into a doorway, pulling his stem and lighter from his pocket and loading up his pipe. *Flick,* was the sound the lighter made as the large flame brightened the doorway as he beamed up to Scotty. The feeling was like no other as he let it take over his body, standing stuck for a moment than repeating the process. "Click!" Suddenly he heard the sound of a gun cocking and looked up straight into the barrel.

"This is for Shank," the feminine voice said before pulling the trigger.

Boom! Boom!

Hassan exited the store and headed towards his car when he heard shots coming from behind him in the alley. He immediately pulled his hammer out his waist and began busting back. He didn't know who it was that was gunning for him but it didn't matter, everybody wanted to get at the throne. Between the Dopeman Dave's beef and taking over Edenwald, he had amassed his share of enemies. He let off a few more shots then raced around his car, got in and pulled off as the shorty with him screamed at the top of her lungs.

Rhae came down the alley firing. She didn't know who it was shooting at her but after killing Fats her adrenaline was pumping and anybody could get it. She made it to the end of the alley just as the car pulled from in front of the store and let off two shot in its direction as it sped away from the scene. She tightened the strings on her hoodie and disappeared back down the alley unseen. She thought killing Fats would make her feel gratified, exacting revenge for Shank but it hadn't, she still felt the empty void of not having her mentor around. Only his freedom could make that feeling she felt go away.

CHAPTER EIGHT

1987

The line in front of the club was wrapped around the corner, as a line of luxury cars circled the block continuously like a carousel. The entire city had come out to celebrate with Hassan, as he welcomed his right hand man, Papo, home. It had be 7 long years since Papo seen the streets and much had changed including the drug of choice and Hassan's position in the game. His whole team was getting money and he couldn't wait to integrate Papo back into the fold. The club was packed as the crew entered and the DJ announced their presence. It truly was unnecessary, all eyes had been on them anyway. The dance floor was full as guys and girls danced to the latest hip hop records. Hassan posted against the wall taking in the whole atmosphere with Papo to his right. The look of amazement on Papo's face said it all, his man had really taken over while he was gone, like they always planned. There were hustlers from every borough in the building but no one outshined Hassan or his crew and they knew it. Some came up and greeted him with pounds, daps and handshakes. Others hated from a distance, while keeping a closer tab on their women now that he had arrived.

"Welcome home to my nigga Papo," the DJ shouted over the mic then shined the spotlight their way. "I see my nigga Hassan in here."

Papo just nodded then turned to Hassan, "Yo, you really got it like that God." Papo's demeanor was much calmer than before he went to jail but he was still a livewire. He had been forced to mature behind the wall but jail had also made him more vicious. Being raised around gladiators will do that. He had taken on the beliefs of the 5 Percent Nation, now he started most his sentences with "Peace" and ended them in "God." But he was far from Godly and didn't try his best to keep the peace either.

"You ain't seen nothing yet B," Hassan said as he motioned for everybody to follow him to VIP.

When they walked through the valet ropes, Hassan spotted Eric B & Rakim and introduced his crew to them. After a few minutes of small talk, they walked to their section. There were 20 bottles of Moet on the tables and pretty women waiting on them. Hassan had pulled out all the stops to welcome his man home.

"Welcome home my nigga! Have fun," Hassan said as he pushed Papo towards the table of ladies. "Ladies meet the man of the night."

Throughout the night Hassan introduced different movers and shakers to Papo, including members of the crew that he wasn't familiar with and some he knew from back in the day.

"So tell me how you got this shit running, niggas coming up north telling me you the man and shit. I'm ready to jump in with both feet and get some of this money you throwin' around in here. I see you getting' it God. You shinin' like a star, big truck jewelry around your neck, four finger rings, big boy Benz outside."

"You remember that nigga Dopeman Dave?" Hassan leaned in and whispered.

"Hell yeah," Papo said.

"Well he ain't around no more," he said as he made a slashing motion across his throat. "I knocked that nigga out the box with the help of my nigga Frog. You remember him right, Maxine brotha."

Papo's face immediately frowned up, "Frog from the Southside. You always did fuck with that nigga back in the day. You know I don't fuck with none of them Southside niggas," Papo quickly made his stance clear.

"Times have changed my nigga, I got the whole projects united, ain't no more of that Northside, Southside beefin'. We all one now baby boy. I get the bricks from El Jefe, supply the spots on the north and south. I got Birdie running the north and Frog running south. Shit run smooth as a baby's ass. And I want to keep it like that, you feel me?" he said letting Papo know that he needed to roll with the rush. "Where I wanna bring you in is on the security side, you put you a little team together and y'all handle all beefs. Anybody that try to move on the team y'all squash 'em immediately. Make sure the spots ain't getting' robbed, you know shit like that. Now how you get your money is," he paused briefly. "You gonna get a percentage off of what every spot makes each week. That way you should be able to feed you and your crew properly." Hassan had just put his right hand man in a position to make more money than anybody else in the crew. He felt it was only right, he and Papo went back since day one. Hassan knew he had a nigga on his team that was like his brother and he trusted more than anyone. He believed in letting his crew eat, "You either feed the wolves or the wolves feed off of you," he believed in his heart.

Papo took a swig of Moet, then put the bottle down on the table. "That's cool," he said dapping Hassan up. "That'll work for now."

Rhae entered the club and immediately turned heads. She was wearing a white spandex body suit, with red knee high boots and a custom made red Gucci leather jacket. She rocked her hair to one side with her bang covering her eye slightly and gold door knocker earrings with her name in them. She was definitely a fly girl and she knew it. Rhae strutted through the club towards the bar, pulling her arm away from a few guys who tried to get her attention on her way. She knew the bar was the place to be, she could survey the whole spot, seeing who was coming and going. But she also knew she wouldn't have to spend a dime all night, cause plenty of dudes would be dying to buy her drinks just for a moment of her time. Rhae squeezed into a spot at the bar, took a seat and waited for the bartender to approach. Once he did she ordered a Sex on the Beach and before she could pay, a guy a few seats over got the bartender's attention and offered to pay for her drink. Rhae just laughed to herself, it was always that easy for her.

She sat sipping on her drink and waited for the guy to make his way over to her. She knew the routine and already had her lines in her head to let him down easy. She nodded her head to the music. The DJ was jamming tonight playing all the hot records she liked. Rhae didn't roll with a crew of girls, preferring instead to fly solo. She never wanted to take the risk of a chick playing herself and it reflecting badly on her, so she didn't do homegirls.

"Can you send some more bottles to our table, and get shorty right here another one of whatever it is that she drinking," a voice from behind her shouted over the loud music causing her to turn in her stool.

Standing directly behind her was a handsome, well built, Puerto Rican with a wavy fade and a fat rope chain. Papo had made his way through the crowd to order some bottles because their waitress was taking too long.

"Thank you," she said with a smile. "But you didn't have to…"

"It's no problem," he said. "What's your name shorty?"

"Rhae," she said with a smile.

"Ray? Like Sugar Ray, the boxer?" he asked confused.

"Pronounced the same, spelled different," she explained.

"Ok, that's definitely different but I like it. It makes you stand out," Papo flirted.

"Thank you," she said.

"You here by yourself?" Papo asked. He didn't care if she was with somebody, she was fly and he liked her.

"Yeah, I'm by myself," Rhae replied.

"Won't you grab that drink right there and come back to VIP with me. It's way more comfortable than being stuck at the bar with dudes hounding you all night," he offered.

"You know what," she said before sipping the last of her drink and picking up the new one Papo had ordered for her. "I think I'll will."

Rhae and Papo walked through the valet ropes into VIP. The party beyond the ropes was much different than what was going on inside the other parts of the club. The rules that applied to the rest of the spot didn't seem to apply once you pass through the ropes and curtains. Guys and girls partied harder, there were some tables with lines of coke on them and people getting high. Another table two girls kissed and groped each other while a dude tossed money on them. Rhae wondered what she had gotten herself into and thought about turning around as Papo led her to his section.

When the two of them arrived, Rhae was happy not to see a similar scene to what was going on in the rest of VIP, but there were a bunch of groupie females and hanger-ons in Papo's section.

"Anything that's here you can have," Papo said pointing to all the liquor on the tables.

"And if you want a lil' something else," he said flicking his nose with his thumb letting her he meant some nose candy. "You just let me know shorty. This is my party, I can make it happen," he bragged.

Rhae just shook her head but didn't plan on taking him up on his offer. She didn't do anything but drink, drugs weren't her thing at all. Rhae looked around at all the dudes with gold rings and chains and immediately knew she was in the midst of a group of drug dealers, And from the looks of it, they had money to burn.

"Enjoy yourself shorty," Papo said. "You with Papo, everything good." He was feeling himself. Fresh out of jail, surrounded by beautiful women and champagne, this was the life he always dreamed of.

Suddenly Papo was pulled away by Birdie and given another bottle as the two of them went and mingled with the rest of the group. Rhae stood there looking out of place as everybody danced to the music and talked amongst themselves.

After a few minutes of standing there and sipping on her drink, she decided this wasn't the scene for her and she was ready to bounce. Papo had brought her to VIP but quickly disappeared. He was freshly home and wasn't trying to be stuck talking to one woman all night, he wanted to keep his options open. Rhae seen the writing on the wall.

"How are you doing?" a voice from over her shoulder asked.

When she turned, Hassan stood there and she almost choked on her drink at how fine he was. His green eyes captured her immediately, they were so hypnotizing. His smooth style put her in mind of Big Daddy Kane as he smiled at her with a perfect set of pearly whites, which seemed even whiter against his skin tone.

"Why you just standing over here by yourself, looking all stiff," he asked.

"I was invited by the guy whose party this is but he disappeared on me," she said. Staring at the man standing in front of her, she had already pushed Papo out of her mind.

Hassan just shook his head, Papo was bugging out. He was chasing as many women as he could, but he might have missed out on the baddest one, at least from where Hassan was standing. Shorty was fly and her style was fresh, not to mention her body suit hugged every curve of her body showing her nice shape.

"What's your name?" Hassan asked.

"Rhae," she answered, prepared to explain like she had done with Papo. But to her surprise she didn't.

"I like that, that's different and it's dope," he charmed. "I'm Hassan, nice to meet you Rhae," he said extending his hand, shaking her hand gently then holding it for a second before letting it go. "Come have a seat," he offered leading her to one of the couches.

Rhae followed him, the name Hassan was familiar to her. His name rang bells in the streets and if he was who she thought he was, she was dealing with a boss. Papo was just fronting, Hassan was the real thing. He motioned for a couple of his henchmen to move so they could sit down, they didn't hesitate, quickly clearing out. Rhae knew then for sure that this was the man she had heard all about. She sat down and he did too, close to her but not too close for comfort. His cologne entered her nostrils and she took in the intoxicating smell, there was nothing she liked more than a good scent on a man. He was gaining points with her by the second.

"What you sippin' on?" he asked looking at her half empty drink.

"Sex on the Beach," she said.

"You want anotha one?" he asked.

"No I'm good for now," Rhae replied.

"So where you from shorty? Cause I ain't never seen you around before."

Suddenly shots rapidly rang out in the club, leaving Rhae stuck and unable to answer. Hassan covered her up, placing his body on top of hers and waited for the shots to stop. Two rival crews were having a shootout inside the club. Innocent bystanders were being hit as well as the dealers the shots were meant for. When there was a break in the shots Hassan grabbed Rhae by the hand and told her to follow him out the back exit. She did as he said and they made it outside the club through the emergency exit and so did the rest of the crew.

"You ok?" Hassan turned to Rhae and asked while still holding her hand.

"Yes I'm fine," she said a little shook up and out of breath.

"Where'd you park?" he asked.

"Two blocks over," she answered.

"C'mon I'll give you a ride to your car," he said as his crew made their way to the vehicles as well, sirens could be heard in the back speeding towards the scene at the club.

Hassan started up his car and pulled out of his parking spot. "You sure you alright?" he questioned once again. Just looking over at her he could see she was shook up but was trying to keep it together. Hassan admired her toughness.

"Yeah, I'll be fine," she said.

"I don't feel like we got a chance to really get to

know each other before niggas started getting busy in there," he confessed. "I would really like to get to know you, maybe somewhere a lil' safer. Maybe we can go to the library or somethin'," he joked causing her to smile.

"I don't see why that would be a problem," she answered.

They exchanged numbers and Hassan promised to call as he dropped her off at her car. He stayed until she made it into her car safely, started her engine and pulled off.

Papo, who had been following Hassan's car the whole time making sure he was good, pulled up on the side of him and rolled his window down. "It's like that my nigga?" he questioned.

"Da fuck you talkin' bout," he spat back.

"You just gonna bag my bitch like that?" Papo asked.

Hassan just chuckled. "You wasn't sweatin' shorty like that," he said referring to the fact Papo had two females in his car. "Plus you know the game, ya bitch chose me," Hassan cracked causing the both of them to laugh.

"I'm just fuckin' with you my nigga," Papo said laughing.

"Welcome home my nigga, go enjoy ya self," Hassan nodded than sped off.

Rhae cruised through the streets on her way to her apartment. She was beat. All the excitement from the night's events had her adrenaline rushing but now that it was coming down because she kept yawning as she drove. Hassan was on her mind the entire ride. She had the feeling of a school girl with a crush and if it hadn't been for her sleepiness she would have been able to show her excitement.

Rhae brought her car to a stop at a red light and waited for it to turn green. Her constant yawning was making her eyes water and she reached into her glove box to get some tissue. When she opened the compartment her gun fell out on to the floor and she stretched down to pick it up. She was able to grab and put it back, just as she seen the reflection for the stop light turn green. She quickly sat up straight and pressed on the gas, only to have to slam on her brake at the person crossing the street in front of her car. Rhae screamed as she almost his the pedestrian, then honked her horn. The person looked into the car, then quickly walked across the street.

Rhae couldn't believe her eyes, she just stayed

parked at the light until it turned red again as she watched the woman walk up the block. Cars behind her started honking when the light finally turned green again hoping that she would go. Finally, she snapped out of her daze and turned in the direction the lady had walked. As she got on the block she eased her car up next to the lady and got an even closer look at her. Rhae's worst fears were confirmed, it was Charlene and she was strung out on crack. She looked like she had been up for a couple of nights and had the appearance of a working girl. Tears formed in Rhae's eyes as she pulled over and parked and jumped out her car. Charlene noticing the same car that had almost hit her had been following her, turned and began to walk the opposite way.

"Charlene, Charlene," Rhae called out to her stopping her in her tracks. "Charlene, it's me Rhae."

Hearing Rhae's name, Charlene immediately felt embarrassed and ashamed at what she had become. She couldn't even turn to face the girl she called her little sister.

"Charlene don't run, please. I miss you, I just want to talk to you," Rhae cried out tears rolling down her face.

Charlene finally turned to face Rhae allowing her

to see what the drug had done to her. She looked bad and Rhae could see she had been in the streets for a long time. But the more she stared at her the more she was able to see glimpses of her once beautiful sister even through all the prostitute make-up.

"Hi Rhae," Charlene said in a low tone keeping her head down staring at the ground. "How you been?"

Rhae couldn't control her emotions as she tried to speak through her tears. "Please Charlene let me help you, let me get you off the street and help you get clean," Rhae begged.

"Do you want to get clean?"

"Yes," Charlene said as she finally looked up from the ground.

"Ok," Rhae said as her mind raced trying to come up with a plan on the spot. "Ok come with me. You can stay at my house tonight. Then in the morning we can get you into a program," Rhae said as she put her arms around Charlene and walked her back to her car.

CHAPTER NINE

Rhae was emotionally drained after spending the weekend trying to find a drug treatment facility that would accept her sister. Charlene didn't make it easy on her either, she tried a couple of times to escape Rhae's apartment, hoping to hit the street to feed her need for a hit. The weekend was hell for the both of them but Rhae refused to give up on her and when she pulled away from the rehab she was finally able to breathe a sigh of relief. She knew Charlene had a long road ahead of her but she had taken the first step on her road to recovery and Rhae was going to do whatever she could to help her.

Now home alone, she looked around at her apartment and realized that she had been neglecting it over the past week. Rhae decided to give it a thorough cleaning, something she enjoyed doing. Cleaning her placed always reminded her of where she came from and gave her a sense of pride in how far she had come. Living in the streets as a runaway she would dream at night about having her own place and how she would decorate it. And that was exactly what she did. Her apartment looked like it did in her dreams.

Rhae was scrubbing down the bathtub when she heard the house phone ringing. She removed her yellow gloves and raced towards the front of the apartment to answer.

"Hello," she said picking up the sounding out of breath.

"What up Rhae, this Hassan, you busy?" he asked in his smooth but rugged tone.

"Just doing some house work, but you give me a reason to take a much needed rest," she said smiling into the phone happy that he called.

"Cleanliness is next to godliness, you tell a lot about a woman by how she keep her crib," he said.

"That's not necessarily true," Rhae replied. "She

could have a spotless home and have still have dirty ways."

"Is that a warning?" he asked jokingly. "Now you got me second guessing what I called for."

"Maybe you should," she said sarcastically than bust out laughing. Rhae found their verbal tennis match funny. Not only was Hassan good looking and street but he had a sense of humor, something Rhae really liked.

"What you got going on tonight?" he asked. "I wanted to come scoop you and hangout. Hopefully show you a better time than the last."

"What time you did you have in mind?" she easily accepted his offer.

"Round 7," he said.

"Ok."

"Aight I'll see you than," he said before hanging up.

✳✳✳

Hassan hung up the large grey cell phone he had installed in his car and suddenly the car went quiet. The only sound was from the wipers going back and forth keeping the rain off the windshield allowing him to watch his money. Hassan was parked in the cut out of plain sight like usual. He studied the comings and goings, in and out of the projects as cars pulled up to cop crack from the pitchers serving out in the open in front of one of the buildings. The projects were in a prime location for upper class drug addicts who lived in suburban Westchester. They no longer had to travel deep into the city to score. Hassan's growing empire gave them quick access to the high they so desperately craved and they brought tons of cash with them. The young drug lord had a cash cow but when you dealing with a straight cash enterprise you have to keep an even closer eye on your money. No matter how much you feed people, greed tends to creep in and they always want more. That was the case as Hassan watched one of his workers constantly going back and forth to his stash then serving the cars. Hassan had suspected he was double dealing, meaning he was serving customers with something other than Hassan's work.

"You see this nigga," Hassan said pointing the hustler out to Papo. "This the type of shit that I need you to be handling. This nigga double dealing," Hassan explained pulling a vial of crack from his pocket holding it up for Papo to see. "I got this from somebody I sent to him to cop. Nigga selling blue tops to my customers cutting himself in on my money," he voiced his frustrations. "Gotta mash that out, that stealing shit is like an infection it will spread quickly amongst these niggas if it's not handled ASAP. You feel me?"

Papo wore his black bucket hat pulled down low over his eyes, and just nodded as he watched the pitcher continuously dart back and forth. "I got chu god," he said. "That's some sucker shit, and we won't have none of dat inside this crew."

"Exactly, I don't wanna see that nigga no more. Put one of ya niggas on it and get that done," Hassan said reaching his hand out giving Papo a pound.

"What you getting into tonight with my chick?" Papo teased.

"Haha," Hassan couldn't help but laugh at his man. "I'm gonna take shorty to A.C. Tyson fighting this weekend."

"Atlantic City," Papo nodded his arrival. "Do ya thang," he said dapping his man back.

"I'ma handle that nigga for you tho. Peace, god," Papo said before jumping out the car into the rain and jogging to his car while Hassan pulled off.

✳✳✳

"So I'm clearly underdressed for the occasion," Rhae said as Hassan stood in her doorway holding an umbrella, dressed in all black slacks, a dress shirt and Gucci loafers. Gone was the big jewelry he sported the night they met in the club. Today he was more understated, choosing to wear just a gold Rolex on his wrist. Rhae liked how he cleaned up.

"Nah, you alright," he said smiling as he looked her up and down.

"Where we going anyway?" she asked as he walked her to the car using the umbrella to shield them from the rain.

"To the Tyson fight in Atlantic City," he said winking at her and smiling before closing the car door behind her.

Rhae looked as if she could kill him when he got in the car but he refused to look her way instead he just smiled started the car. She was in no way prepared or dressed to go to an event like that. And she was not about to be caught dead at the fight looking raggedy.

"No, no, no," she protested as Hassan continued to avoid eye contact. "See you too slick for your own good. You know you wrong that's why you so quiet. You could have told me where we was going then I could have..."

"What, gotten dressed up?" he said finally looking

over towards her. "That would've ruined the surprise. Trust me I know the importance of looking and feeling your best. And I wouldn't have you out looking anything less. Just trust me on this one," he said smoothly.

"You asking a lot for someone I just met," she said sarcastically then her evil look was replaced with a smile.

"Now I see why you ain't got no man," he joked back with her.

"How you know I don't," she shot back unwilling to let him get the last word in.

"If you do, you won't much longer when he see your ass sitting next to me on HBO, ringside," he said pulling the two tickets out the visor and handed them to her. "Yeah, I bet you just broke up wit' him in your mind," Hassan said finally able to shut her down.

The two of them got to know each other during the two hour ride down to Atlantic City, talking the entire time and seemed disappointed when they pulled into the valet parking area at the Trump Plaza. They quickly checked in and were escorted to one of the high roller suites on the top floor of the casino. Rhae was extremely impressed by the luxurious setting as she toured the suite.

"Rhae," Hassan called out from the living room area. "Rhae, this is Liza, she is with the consignor services of the hotel. She is gonna be like your own personal assistant. I scheduled a car service to come pick you up and take you shopping anywhere you want to go to get whatever you need. So you can look and feel your best. Liza is gonna help you with that. Is that cool?" he asked a shocked Rhae. Hassan was really a boss and she was digging his take charge attitude.

"Ok," she answered.

Hassan disappeared into the room then reappeared holding 5 thousand dollars wrapped in a rubber band and handed it to her. "This should be enough," he said then winked. "Have fun, when you come back we gonna do some gambling."

Hassan watched the two women disappear out the door, then quickly returned to the room. He walked over to the safe in the room and punched in the code cracking it opening. He grabbed the black leather duffle bag off the bed and removed 50 thousand dollars, placing it in the safe than closing it. He zipped the duffle bag back up and place it over his shoulder then exited the front door of the suite. Making his way to the opposite end of the hall, he knocked on another room door. After a few seconds, the door opened up and there stood El Jefe. The two men embraced and Hassan walked in.

"Hey what you drinking?" El Jefe asked.

"Whatever you pouring," Hassan said.

"Champagne, I'm drinking champagne all night. I got a good feeling about this fight tomorrow night. Tyson is going down," he proclaimed.

"Yeah," Hassan said giving his connect a suspicious look.

"You know I hear things," El Jefe said pointing to his ears. "Tyson has been partying a lot, not training like he should. Chasing pussy all night. He's going down," he laughed. "Anyway what's in the bag," he said quickly turning the conversion to business.

Hassan handed him the bag. El Jefe unzipped it and looked in it see nothing but dead presidents staring back at him. He closed the bag back up, never bothering to count it. Hassan's money was always precise and El never had to question that. "So your guy is downstairs?" he asked.

"Yeah, he's downstairs in a grey Toyota Cressida. Your guys can bring it to him now," Hassan said having had Birdie follow him to Atlantic City. This was a business trip, no better weekend then to conduct business than under the veil of a big fight.

El Jefe walked over to the phone in the room, pick it up and dialed, then spoke a few words in Spanish before hanging up. "It's done," he said.

Hassan stood to his feet and shook El Jefe's hand. The two men had handled what they needed to so there would be no reason for them to see each other again the rest of the weekend. It also allowed Hassan to focus all his attention on getting to know Rhae and showing her a good time.

Papo and one of his young henchmen ascended the stairwell in the projects, passing a few fiends on their way down from copping in the process. The closer they got to the top floor the darker it become in the stairwell as they started to hear voices clearer. Papo paused trying to make out the voices. He wanted to know exactly how many people were up at the top of the next flight of stairs. After listening for a few minutes he realized it was three niggas and pulled out his gun, his henchmen did the same as they continued creeping up on the unsuspecting trio. Papo had heard that when the kid who was double dealing finished his shift in front of the buildings, this is where he got off his blue tops, right under the crew's nose. He was in direct violation and had to be dealt with.

Papo tucked his gun in his pants and pulled his hat down over his eyes some. "Stay right here. You got them other niggas? I'ma send em right to you," he said to his henchmen.

Papo stumbled up the steps like he had been drinking, slurring his speech as he reached the two dudes at the bottom of the stairs.

"Yo hold up my man, what up doing?" one of the pitchers said placing his hand on Papo's chest and the other hand on his gun.

"I heard y'all got them $5 blue tops. That's all, I don't want no problems," Papo said knowing for sure that the kid didn't recognize him.

"Yo, send that nigga up the steps," Papo's main target yelled from the top of the flight of stairs. Papo walked up the stairs and stood in front of the kid who then asked, "What you need?"

"All of it," Papo said lifting his hat off his face and his gun at the same time. The two niggas at the bottom of the steps were already being held at gun point by Papo's young henchmen who had crept up silently on them. The young hustler begged for his life but Papo wouldn't hear none of it, he went in his pockets and took his money. The door to the roof suddenly swung up startling Papo and without hesitating he turned and pulled the trigger.

Boom! Boom!

Two shots hit the man coming through the door in the chest laying him on his back. The flashlight that was in the man's hand hit the ground and rolled down the steps and came to a stop at Papo's feet. It was then he was able to see from the light of the door being opened, that he had shot by a housing officer who was doing his routine patrol of the stairways and the roof. The brief distraction gave the young hustler marked for death the chance to escape and he took full advantage of the opportunity. Papo nor his henchmen gave chase, instead they both ran the opposite way, trying to get away from the murder they had just committed.

CHAPTER TEN

"Yo, this nigga bodied a cop?" Hassan barked into the car phone as he sat parked in front of Rhae's apartment. He had to cut their weekend trip short and she could tell from his clenched jaw the entire ride home that something was wrong. She didn't press him about it, choosing instead to remain mostly silent during the drive. He had just dropped her off, walked her to the door of her building and made sure she got inside safe, when he returned to call Birdie.

"Yeah, this nigga dropped a housing officer and ain't even hit the kid he was supposed to," Birdie replied.

"Yo this nigga just made the hood hot, too hot to get any type of money. I need the spots shut down for a few days. Move shit to the spots outside the projects. Cause trust they coming," Hassan's frustration was on display. "Just gotta let shit cool down, then we'll start opening back up a few at a time. Get the word to Frog and them, I need everything shut down on both sides no later than tonight," he informed.

"No doubt," Birdie said before hanging up.

Hassan immediately beeped Papo and waited from him to call back. He had to speak with him and find out what went wrong. Since Papo been home he's been handling the security and enforcement side of the business for the crew and hadn't come close to fucking up like this. So Hassan needed to hear his side of the story. Shit was about to get crazy for the crew. He knew the cops would come at them full force for taking one of theirs, if they were able to figure out who was responsible. NYPD was the biggest gang in the city and you didn't want to be in their crosshairs. Hassan knew he had to get rid of anybody that could place Papo in that staircase or all hell was gonna break loose.

Hassan picked up the phone on the first ring. "Yo, don't say nothing," he said quickly to Papo not wanting to discuss what happened over the phone. "Meet me on B Road at the lil' bar on the corner," then he hung up.

Pulling up just down the block from the bar, he parked and took his gun out the stash spot before hopping out. He walked up the block and entered the little hole in the wall bar. The spot was where older bingo playing cats frequented to drink and talk shit. It was his first time there, but he knew it was the last place he would be expected, perfect to meet Papo. There might have been four customers in the whole place when he entered, so he grabbed one of the many empty stools at the very end of the bar. The bartender was an older, medium built, brown skinned man with a thick mustache that looked like it belonged in the 70's. Hassan watched the man interact with the men already seated around the bar and from their conversation he was able to figure out the man was the owner. After a few minutes he made his way over to Hassan, wiping the bar down in front of him then placing a coaster down.

"What'll it be?" he asked.

"Bacardi and coke," Hassan said.

"I've never seen you in here before," the man said making small talk as he made the drink. "I never forget a face," he said.

"That's a good skill to have," Hassan replied.

"Tell me about it," the man said cracking a smile.

Hassan paid and tipped him then sat sipping his drink while he waited for Papo to show his face. He needed to tie up all the loose ends behind Papo's fuck up, he wanted anyone that could point the finger at his crew in the ground. He knew that the kid who had been double dealing would be the first to cooperate with police after the botched attempt on his life. He had been green lighted and would be looking for refuge from the cops. Hassan checked his watch, growing impatient. He began looking around taking in the all the sports memorabilia on the walls, admiring all the trophies and pictures behind the bar. As he surveyed the photos one caught his eye and made a lump form in his throat. The picture hung right over the cash register. It was a picture of the bartender with his arm around Samantha, the young girl Papo had accidently shot when they were teenagers. The resemblance was undeniable; the man was her father. Not a day went by that Hassan didn't think about the incident on the roof that took her life and now he had walked into her father's bar. He downed his drink in one gulp, reached in his pocket pulling out a one-hundred-dollar bill and placed the empty glass on it on top of the bar. There was no way he could have Papo meet him at that bar. He stood up off the stool, just as the Samantha's father made his way back over to him.

"Can I get you anything else?" he asked.

"No thanks, you have a good one," Hassan said as he nodded, turned and walked towards the door.

Boom! Boom! Boom!

Hassan heard the shots before he felt the burning sensation in his shoulder and back and knew he had been shot. Samantha's father had recognized him. When you lose a child you never forget the faces of the people involved and he hadn't either. Hassan placed his hand on the ground like a running back would to keep his balance, so he wouldn't fall. He knew if he hit the ground he wouldn't make it out of there alive. His left shoulder was hanging at his side and was in excruciating pain. Hassan managed to pull his gun, turned and fired off a couple shots. His aim was off and the shots went wild missing the man but shattering the glass mirror behind the bar bringing down the shelves of liquor. Hassan darted out the front door bleeding everywhere as he made it to his car. He jumped in, started it up and pulled out into traffic burning rubber.

Rhae was still unpacking when she heard someone banging on her door like they were trying to knock it off the hinges. She looked over at her landlord, Ms. Shelton, who had stopped by to pick up the rent and see how she was liking the apartment. Both women had a startled look on their faces as the person continued to bang on the door. Rhae stalked over to the door angry and embarrassed in front of her landlord. "Who is it?" she shouted.

"Rhae it's me, Hassan," the voice called out from the other side of the door. She looked through the peephole than hurried up and opened the door seeing him bleeding in her hallway.

"Oh my God! What happened?" she asked as he stumbled into her house.

"I got shot," he said breathing heavily.

"Oh my God," Ms. Shelton screamed seeing him bleeding.

"Hassan where? Where are you hit?" Rhae asked in a bit of a panic.

"In my arm and back," he said collapsing to the floor. The loss of blood had him feeling weak.

"He needs to go to the hospital," Ms. Shelton cried

out.

"No hospitals," he yelled. "Who is that?" Hassan said looking up at the older looking woman sporting a fur coat and nice set of pearls.

"She's my landlord," Rhae explained the unfamiliar face.

"Oh," he said still wishing she would shut up. "I got a doctor that can come stitch me up. His number is in my wallet. Get it and call him for me please."

Rhae reached in his pocket and retrieved the number from his wallet. She disappeared into the bathroom then returned with a few towels and attempted to hand them to her landlord.

"Oh no I'm outta here," Ms. Shelton said heading out the door.

Rhae tied one of the towels around his arm near where the bullet had entered and then raced over to the house phone and dialed the doctor's number. She explained who she was calling for and gave her address then hung up.

CHAPTER ELEVEN

Rhae refused to let Hassan leave her apartment after he got shot, so now it had been about two weeks since the incident and he was at her place being willingly captive. Rhae served as a great nurse amongst other things. She and Hassan spent most of every day together, Rhae made sure she didn't leave his side unless it was utterly important. After two days of unanswered pages from Papo, Hassan decided to call him and put him on to the current events. He didn't tell him where he was but assured him he was good and recovering with the best help provided.

"Yo, you want me to go handle that old head for

you?" asked Papo referring to Samantha's father. "You know I'll gladly put the reaper on that ma'fucka, send him to rock with his daughter nah'mean," Papo said anxiously.

Hassan wasn't at all intrigued by anything Papo was saying. Instead he was more disappointed by his friend's cold heart "Nah B, let that man breathe, you understand me?" Hassan knew that if it was him and his child's life being taken, he would eagerly await the day to avenge their death. Therefore, he silently respected what he did. "Shit is hot Papo, I'm out of commission for a minute but the money don't stop. I need you to make sure shit moving smooth for a couple days I'll be good in a couple days."

"I got you my nigga. You just get better eat some soup or some shit!" Papo clowned.

"Yea aight nigga you just be cool no funny shit Papo."

"I'm cool like I be cool baby. I'ma get wit you later, peace god," Papo replied.

"Peace." Hassan hung up the phone and looked up at the beauty that was in the kitchen fixing breakfast.

"Everything okay?" Rhae spoke with her back towards him. She acted as if she was not listening to his conversation by clanking pots and pans around the kitchen but she couldn't help it.

"Everything is all good Pretty. What you burning over there?"

"Ha, burning? You should never insult the person taking care of you," Rhae snapped back before placing a plate of grits, cheese eggs and sausages in front of him.

"Damn this plate is fit for a king. You've done well now let's see if it tastes as good as it looks," Hassan replied flirtatiously never taking his eyes of Rhae.

"You just eat your food and get your strength back so I can whip your ass in this game of pity pat," Rhae shot back as she picked up the deck of cards on the table.

"You don't want that problem," Hassan chuckled while stuffing a spoonful of grits in his mouth. "My moms used to have me up with her in the kitchen 'til the wee hours of the morning, while she cracked heads in pity pat. She sent all her friends home mad as hell with empty pockets. I was her good luck charm, as she liked to call me. She schooled me well to the game Miss Lady," Hassan reminisced, taking a trip down memory lane. He rarely talked about his mother to anyone but somehow felt comfortable around Rhae to tell her about his childhood.

"Your mom huh? You light up when you talk about her. Are you two still close?" Rhae asked.

"Not as we should be but she my ol'lady tho. I wouldn't trade her," Hassan replied.

Rhae noticed Hassan's face change from happiness to hurt within seconds of speaking of her. "Is she okay? Your mother that is," Rhae asked.

"She's better now, streets had her in a choke hold. She getting it right now tho," Hassan said confidently.

Rhae walked around the table to where Hassan was sitting and rubbed her hand across his back. "It's time to change the dressing on your wound," she said trying to change the subject a little bit, noticing how it kind of brought down Hassan's spirit. Hassan reached his arm around, grabbing her hand and pulled her close to him between his legs. Rhae's heart suddenly skipped a beat being that close to Hassan. His chest was bare and he only wore some sweat pants. His body was perfect wounded and all and the thump she felt in her panties confirmed that her body agreed with her mind.

"Why you take care of me so good?" he said breaking her out of her impure thoughts.

"What chu mean? Because you need taken care of, you're hurt."

"Nah you do it like you care, not like a public service. My mom was the only lady that ever cared," Hassan answered sincerely.

"Maybe cause I do," she immediately said surprising herself and causing Hassan to smile.

He stood up towering over her cupped her face and kissed her lips. Hassan's full lips covered hers naturally but felt perfect in the connection. Rhae's nipples hardened from the unexpected kiss but she welcomed it freely. "Get dressed," Hassan said breaking the moment.

"Huh," Rhae was caught off guard by what he said. She was caught in the moment and honestly didn't want it to end. His kiss was gentle and soft, she wanted more.

"I said get dressed. I'm taking you somewhere," he repeated.

Snapping back to reality, Rhae took a step back. "You're hurt Hassan. Where do you think you're going? You can't drive in your condition," Rhae said.

"I'm not, you are. You can follow directions right?" Hassan said jokingly.

"Oh you got jokes, huh?"

"I'm saying some people only know how to give em. I don't know, you might be one of those people," they both shared a laugh. "I'ma shower then you can change my bandage. Then we can roll out. How that sound?"

Rhae couldn't lie, she was used to giving out directions but was truly intrigued by what Hassan had up his sleeve, so she was willing to do what he asked. "Okay," she answered.

He lifted her chin and kissed her lips again before he retreated to the bathroom. Rhae wasn't sure if she was ready to accept the feeling she got from being around Hassan. He was fun and sexy, not to mention she felt free. She was able to be herself around him, completely unguarded. In every sense she wanted to feel uncomfortable with that feeling but for some reason she couldn't. It felt natural, she felt like she belonged.

They pulled into the driveway a nice size home in the upstate city of Peekskill. The house that belonged to Hassan's grandfather and was still in the family. Rhae had never been this far upstate and liked the look of the area, it was so different than anything she was used to. She admired the middle class look of the neighborhood.

"This looks like a good place to raise a family," she

said.

"Don't let it fool you," Hassan said as he got out the car. "C'mon," he said to her smiling.

"Whose house is this?" she asked as she got out, looking up at the beautiful home.

"This was my grandfather's house, now it belongs to me," he informed her as she followed him onto the porch. "My mother lives here," he said with a sheepish grin as he reached out and rang the doorbell.

"Your mother?" she said with a surprised look on her face. "I'm gonna kill you," she mumbled under her breath as the door swung open.

Rhae was taken aback by what she saw, Hassan's mother was all skin and bones and looked like if a strong gust of wind blew through, it would knock her over. Rhae could immediately tell that she was sick and from the story Hassan had told her, she realized that his mother must had contracted AIDS during her days running in the streets.

"What are you doing out of bed ma?" Hassan asked seeing her struggling to hold herself up. "Where's your nurse?" he asked.

"Boy, hush," she spoke with a raspy voice. "I wanted to see who this pretty girl you got standing next to you was," she said mustering up a smile.

"Ma, this is Rhae, Rhae this is my mother, Monica," he introduced the two.

"Hi, how are you?" Rhae said extending her hand.

"Aren't you beautiful," Monica said grabbing Rhae and hugging her. "You must be special, Hassan never introduced me to any of his female friends before," she said as she released her from her embrace.

"C'mon ma, chill," Hassan said blushing.

Rhae laughed.

"Boy, don't tell me to chill," she said hitting him in the arm.

"Arrgh," Hassan moaned from the pain.

"What's wrong with your arm?" Monica asked seeing her son in agony.

"I got shot but I'm…"

"What," she said getting excited.

"Calm down ma, I'm okay. Rhae has been taking good care of me," Hassan said with all his charm before walking into the house.

"Thank God somebody is," Monica said.

Rhae did not know how comfortable she was being around Hassan's mother. In her mind all she could think about was what she was wearing and if it was appropriate attire to be around her. She looked down quickly giving herself the once over, while not trying to be obvious. *Oh my God, I hope I look okay,* she thought. *Wait a minute, why do I care? He should not have brought me here anyway. You only bring your girl to see your mother...wait I know he don't think...*

Hassan snapped Rhae out of her thoughts by grabbing her hand. "You thirsty?" he asked.

"Huh," she responded caught off guard. "I can use some water," Rhae then replied.

"Hassan get that pretty girl some lemonade out the refrigerator. You want some lemonade baby?" Monica asked with a smile spread wide across her face trying her best to be hospitable. She didn't have many visitors come see her, outside of Hassan, so she was embracing the new face.

"Oh, no thank you ma'am water is fine," Rhae replied.

"Call me Monica baby," she insisted.

Hassan walked in the kitchen with the two ladies following behind him. "Ma, has Maria been by this week to clean up and refill your meds?" he questioned noticing the sink full of dishes. Maria was the home health aide Hassan hired to help his mother out.

"Three times a week like clockwork," Monica replied sarcastically, she wasn't really a fan of the extra help. "I told her to go home early yesterday. I was feeling okay and moving around just fine, I really didn't need her."

Hassan pulled out both Rhae's and his mother's chair so they could sit before he headed over to the sink to do the dishes. His face showed the displeasure he felt by her last statement. "Ma, you can't send her home," he said shaking his head. "Even if you think you feel well, you need her here at all times," he chastised his mother politely.

Rhae could see how concerned he was for his mother. Though he had mentioned previously that their relationship wasn't as it should be, she could tell he was trying to make up for lost time and savor whatever time they may have left.

Monica brushed her son's comments off and re-focused her attention back to Rhae. "So how'd you wind up with my bad ass son," Monica joked causing both women to burst out laughing.

"I don't know, I'm still asking myself the same thing," Rhae replied looking at Hassan with admiration. Rhae felt a flutter in her chest seeing Hassan with his mother. She didn't have many memories with her parents. The closest thing she had to family was Shank and Charlene and that too was cut short. She admired what he was trying to do. It made her realize that you should cherish what you love the most even if the time spent was cut short. Hassan was from the streets and that was proven, everything about him yelled gangster. But this side of him was rarely seen by anyone, not even those closest to him. So Rhae felt special, even if he hadn't said it, for some reason she knew it. For the rest of the day they sat with Monica watching all her favorite shows. She was happy for the company and Rhae was happy to get a small taste of family life she had always craved. Hassan cleaned the house, the best he could with his injured arm, cooked the ladies dinner and enjoyed their interaction. It was the first time Rhae saw a look of peace on his face, the hard exterior mask was removed and only a woman's son was revealed and a woman's definition of a real man. Hassan had never been more attractive to her than he was at that moment.

CHAPTER TWELVE

Papo sat on the side of the bed and put his gun on the nightstand. He opened the drawer, removing a sandwich bag filled with blue top crack vials. The drugs belonged to the hustler Hassan sent him to kill. The kid had dropped them in the commotion and he picked them up without anybody seeing. Papo had violated the number one rule in the hustler handbook, he had secretly begun to get high off his own supply. He loved the powerful feeling the little white rock gave him when he smoked it. He started out breaking the rock up in his weed when he smoked but recently had started taking straight hits from the pipe. Papo was playing a dangerous game of Russian Roulette with the addictive drug. He told himself no drug was stronger than he was and that he could never be strung out like the fiends he was accustomed to serving. *I just like the feeling but I don't need it,* he told himself every time he would take a blast. But the drug had him in its clutches and its grip only got tighter but he didn't know it yet. He packed his stem then lifted the lighter to take a hit, hearing the rocks spark as they heated up. Inhaling deeply, Papo tilted his head back as the drug entered his lungs. He held the smoke in briefly before exhaling, then laid back on the bed and let the drug take effect. His mind was racing as he contemplated his next move. With Hassan laid up recovering, he was in charge and had something up his sleeve. He knew as long as Hassan was around he wouldn't go along with his plan but with no one to stop him and the drug controlling his thoughts, Papo was ready to put his plan in effect.

The knock at the door made him jump up and grab his gun off the nightstand. He pushed the cracks and the pipe back into the drawer and closed it. His paranoia heightened, the after effect of blasting off. His eyes were wide as a four lane highway and he felt wired. Beads of sweat formed on his forehead as walked to the door, looked through the peephole, and held his gun tightly, ready to shoot anything that moved.

"Who is it?" he yelled out.

"It's us," two voices answered from the other side. "You told us to come through."

"Peace, god," he greeted opening the door and hurrying his two young goons inside. Papo looked out in the hallway to see if they had been followed then closed the door.

"What up god," one of the goons said as he sat down on the couch. "What you needed to holla at us about?"

"I got a move we can make, if y'all down to get some money," Papo said getting straight to the point. He could tell his proposition had intrigued them. They both moved to the edge of their seat on the couch at the mere mention of making money. They were two of his most loyal soldiers and he knew they would be down if he brought them in on his scheme.

"What kind of money you talking?" one of the goons inquired.

Papo saw dollar signs appear in the youngster's eyes. "Big money, no whammies," he kicked it to him. "But you gotta be willing to get it, I don't need n-o suckers on my team," Papo egged on knowing it would tug at the goons manhood.

"I'm down for whatever," the goon spoke up quickly.

"Me too," the other goon chimed in.

"That's what I like to hear," Papo said as he began to pace back and forth in front of them. "Yo, we moving on them Southside niggas, fuck all that peace shit niggas talking. Them niggas Frog and Vel skimming and need to be dealt wit," Papo lied. "I told Hassan them niggas couldn't be trusted. Success breed jealousy and them some disloyal ass niggas. They set up they own boss, for a bigger slice. So it was only a matter of time."

"So Hassan cool with us making a move on them?" one of the goons asked.

"Nigga is you stupid or dumb," Papo shouted. "You not listening to me. I talked to my nigga, he with whatever I'm with, you feel me? I'm in charge of this shit right now. So what I say go," Papo said feeling the rush of power running through his bloodstream.

Papo put his two young goons on Frog. They had been following him for the last two days, tracking his every move and reporting back. Papo knew he didn't have much time to waste, Hassan would be healed shortly and he needed to act now if he was gonna do anything. He wanted to put a bullet in Vel's head as well but running up in the building and killing him wasn't gonna happen. Vel had recruited a strong team to fortify the building his crack spot was in. He had niggas in the front, on the roof and in the back of the building and they all were strapped and ready to kill in an instant. Frog was a much easier target. He moved around much more free flowing than Vel. Frog was a very charismatic hustler, who got his nickname from having big frog eyes. He had nothing but love from everybody in the hood. Hassan always respected Frog's hustle and knew he was the perfect person to help him unite the project because he fucked with everybody and everybody fucked with him. He had an influence on the Southside and Hassan bringing him into the fold made the takeover that much easier. But Papo didn't give a fuck all he saw was a Southside nigga in the position he felt could be his. Nevermind Hassan had set him up financially better than all of his lieutenants and that he gave him his own crew inside of the crew to run. A group of killers and enforcers to handle all the crews beef. Papo was slowly began to manipulate and abuse his position of power. He was turning his group of killers loose on members of his own team. Those he felt were eating too much or he just didn't care for were now on the menu and they didn't even know it.

Frog pulled his Acura Legend up in front of his sister's walk up apartment and grabbed the small leather book bag off the front seat that contained about fifty thousand in cash and a brick of coke. He grabbed his gun from the stash spot in the car, dropped it inside the bag than hopped out the whip. His sister's spot was where he stashed his cash, drugs and guns. She had 2 teenage daughters, so when he offered to move them out the projects and pay her rent in order to use the back room as his own private safe, she quickly agreed.

Frog entered the building and was immediately grabbed and pistol whipped by two masked man waiting in the hallway for him and forced him into his sister's apartment. Papo stood in the middle of the living room wearing a mask with Frog's sister and nieces laying on the floor at gunpoint with their hands tied behind their backs. He only spoke in Spanish as he instructed his henchmen to take Frog in the back room and unlock the safe in the closet. He let him know that he had one shot to enter the combination right or he would kill his sister and nieces who were in tears as they laid bounded on their stomachs. Frog didn't hesitate to cooperate. He didn't keep all his money their anyway and as fast as they were making it, he could replace what he was about to handover in no time. He was more concerned about the safety of his family.

After a few minutes, Frog was led back into the living room at gunpoint and placed on his knees next to his loved ones.

"That's about eighty thousand plus another fifty and a brick in the book bag," Frog said throwing out the figures, hoping it would satisfy the robbers lust for paper. He knew the old saying, "When they masked up they coming for your ice. When they bare-faced they coming for your life," so he felt confident that it would all be over soon.

"Is this all of it?" Papo asked one of the henchmen in Spanish. "You sure?" he quizzed again seeing him nod yes, only to have him nod a second time. Satisfied, Papo pressed his gun right against Frog's forehead and squeezed with no hesitation. He then turned his gun on his three family members tied up on the floor screaming at Frog's dead body lying next to them and emptied his clip into them.

Hassan beeper started to go off with back to back pages with 911 codes. He picked up Rhae's house phone and dialed the number back.

"Yo," he said into the phone hearing it pick up on the other end.

"Turn on the news," Papo said.

Hassan lifted the remote off the bed and flipped to channel 4 and watched as the reporter told about the horrific scene discovered at the Bronx apartment where Frog's sister lived. 3 people were dead, including Frog and one, a fourteen year old girl was said to be in stable condition at a local hospital.

"Meet me in the hood in 20 minutes," Hassan said before hanging up. He stood up and slid on a pair of sweats and stepped into his Timberlands then grabbed the keys off the nightstand. He walked over to the bathroom, stuck his head inside the door, and yelled to Rhae, who was in the shower that he needed to run to the store and would be back. He had recovered enough that she didn't protest and he raced out the door.

Pulling into Edenwald, he parked and hopped out, walking up into the courtyard where members of the MCM awaited. Birdie was there, along with Papo and a few of his goons, as well as Vel and more than a few of his Southside niggas. It seemed like the whole projects was out mourning the death of Frog. He truly had love in the community and the fact that his sister and her kids got caught up in it all wasn't sitting right with anybody in the crew.

"Peace God," Papo said as he greeted Hassan with a pound and embrace. "You good?" he asked referring to his recovery.

"Yeah I'm good," Hassan said as he reached out and began dapping members of the crew up. "Anybody hear anything about the little girl?" he asked. "Is she gonna make it?"

"Yeah she gonna pull through," Vel answered. "One of my chicks was just up at the hospital with Frog's fam. She said shorty gonna be ok."

"Any word on who it was?" Papo asked trying to find out what the girl had told. He was bugging out on the inside not understanding how she lived.

"Not much," Vel answered. "She said they had on mask and was speakin' Spanish."

"That could be a million different ma'fuckas," Hassan said. "Castle Hill, Soundview, wherever. It's Spanish speaking niggas all the over the BX."

"Yo, wasn't Frog fucking with the Dominican

bitch from the South Bronx," Birdie stated.

"Yeah, she was from Mott Haven," Vel said.

"That's King Tito and them," Birdie said.

"She could have set the nigga up," Papo said. "We need to make a move on them niggas," he said amped up trying to persuade Hassan to give the green light.

He was willing to do and say anything to place the attention on anybody other than himself. He had even killed his two henchmen he had used to carry out the murder. He didn't need it getting out that he was responsible and the less people alive that knew the better. Plus he didn't want to split the money with them. So killed them and put them in the truck of a car and left the car under a bridge.

"That is them niggas M.O.," Hassan said rubbing his hand over his chin.

"What's it gonna be Hass?" Birdie asked as Vel and the other Southside hustlers looked on intensively. "We need to get at these niggas."

Hassan knew that if he didn't ride for Frog, he could risk losing the Southside and he couldn't have that. He was making too much money controlling the entire projects. So he made a business decision and greenlighted to move.

"Yo Vel," he called out. "I know where to find

these niggas. Me, you, Bird and Papo gonna handle it," Hassan said.

It was three days before Thanksgiving and the residents in the South Bronx were busy doing what people all over the city did around this time of year. They were preparing for the holidays by visiting family and making runs to the stores, picking up the last items to complete their upcoming Thanksgiving feast. Hassan had different plans as he cruised the streets with his three comrades in two separate sedans, one beige, and one maroon. The street lights glowed a dull yellow as they turned on to Beekman Avenue, a two block stretch in the middle of the Mott Haven neighborhood, ran by King Tito's organization, and rolled up to a narrow alleyway where a group of Dominican dealers were conducting business. The streets were filled with teenagers and the block looked like it was clicking with ten or more people congesting the tiny corridor, some fiends, others workers. Hassan and his henchmen hopped out their cars with murderous intentions and surrounded the spot. Without a warning, Hassan pumped 5 bullets into the stomach and chest of the first Dominican hustler he laid eyes on. His henchmen turned their guns on workers and customers alike and opened fire on the alley not caring who they hit. For the next few minutes there was total chaos and mass confusion as people scrambled to get away from the hail of gunfire filling the small space. Haunting screams filled the air as people on the streets raced for cover as bullets hit the building walls echoing with the deadly stutter associated with automatic weapons. A few were able to escape the gunfire through a hole in a fence at the back of the alley but most were cut down as they tried to flee. One of the men was shot down trying to make his way up a fire escape. Another one of the Dominicans made it out of the alleyway but Birdie chased him fifty feet to the doorway of an adjoining building and shot him eight times. His hand still clung to the doorknob as he laid slumped on the ground. A slim, forty something woman met her fate when she ran out the ally and into Papo's line of fire, taking a bullet to the head. She died in the middle of the sidewalk, still clutching the vial of crack she had just purchased moments before. Hassan's viciousness was on full display as he squeezed until his gun was empty hitting every Dominican he saw. When the shooting stopped, the ground of the alley was painted red with blood. They had sent a clear message that they were not to be fucked with. Hassan back peddled and hopped in his car. Birdie, Vel and Papo did the same as the two cars sped up the block towards E. 141st.

CHAPTER THIRTEEN

Christmas came early for Rhae when she heard a knock at the door. To her surprise Charlene stood in the door looking like her old self. She was beautiful and had put on some weight, all in the right places. Her skin looked radiant and her eyes were full of life. The two women embraced at the door becoming emotional, shedding tears of joy and pain. Charlene had been through hell and back doing things she could have never imagined for a hit of crack. But Rhae went into the fiery pits of hell to drag her out, saving her life in the process.

"Oh my God!" Rhae shouted. "You look beautiful."

"I feel even better," Charlene said as she twirled around with her arms out. "I really didn't think I could do it and I wouldn't have been able to without your help," she confessed.

"But I'm happy to be clean."

"You my sister no matter where life takes us or how far apart we may be, I'll always have your back," Rhae said closing the door behind her. "Come have a seat, we have so much to catch up on."

The two women strutted into the living room and plopped on the couch. Rhae longed to have Charlene back in her life. Their connection was like no other. They had been so close during her younger years and she wanted nothing more than for them to pick up where they had left off. Rhae had so much to tell her about where she had been and things she had done. But what she really wanted to tell her about was the new man in her life. Rhae just wanted some good old fashion girl talk and Charlene wanted the same. It would be the first bit of normalcy she experienced in forever.

"So what have you been up? Tell me everything," Charlene asked.

"Where do you want me to start?" she asked. There was so much to tell. Where would she start?

"Tell me about the nigga that got you up in this fly crib and do he have any friends?" Charlene questioned.

Rhae burst into laughter Charlene hadn't changed a bit. "I got this apartment on my own, nobody helped me do a thang," she said proudly.

Charlene mouth fell open, then she covered it with her hand with a shock look on her face. "You a lesbian," she whispered leaning in towards Rhae. "They got that lil' coochie while you were in that group home. You let them munch on that rug?" Charlene teased.

"Nooo," Rhae said unable to control her laughter. "Hell no, I am strictly dickly girl," she reassured Charlene. "I love men, I just said ain't no nigga put me up in this crib."

"Oh ok, just checking," Charlene said.

"I do have somebody, well somebody I'm seeing," she informed as a smile stretched across her face.

"Do tell," Charlene said moving closer as her interest peaked.

"His name is Hassan, and he is fly. Tall, brown and sex," she bragged.

"Hmmm sounds nice," Charlene said. "When do I get to meet him?"

"Funny you asked," Rhae said. "He throwing a Christmas party this Friday. You can meet him then. And he has friends, plenty of them," she said knowing that would entice Charlene.

"I'm there, I need to be celebrating anyway. I'm happy to be clean and out that fucking rehab. Time to get back on track," she declared.

"You sure? I don't want to put you in an unhealthy situation," Rhae said still concerned for her sister's recovery.

"I'll be fine, Rhae. You'll be there to keep an eye on me as well," she said sarcastically.

At least ten Lincoln Town cars and stretch limousines pulled up back to back, dropping off different members of MCM and their guests. It was a black tie affair and every one was looking their best, dressed to the nines as they prepared to board the private yacht Hassan had chartered for the Christmas party. Top ranking members of the crew like Papo, Birdie and Vel, couldn't resist the chance to show off their new cars, turning down the provided car service. Papo pulled up in a new yellow 300ZX with chrome BBS rims and hopped out in a tuxedo. Birdie and Vel pulled up back to back in 560 SL Mercedes, one black, one red. Never one to be out done, Hassan pulled into the parking lot in a Cocaine white Ferrari Testarossa, with Rhae in the passenger seat. All the attention was on them as they stepped out the car. Hassan wore a white tuxedo jacket, black pants, white dress shirt and black bowtie. Rhae stepped out in a white and black classic jumpsuit and a black fox fur coat. Hassan was the star of the night but he wanted to make sure Rhae's star shined the brightest. Even Charlene couldn't believe how gorgeous Rhae looked. The little girl she protected in the streets was now a full grown woman and had one of the largest niggas in the city on her arm.

"You ready to have a good time?" Hassan stuck his arm out for Rhae.

"Yes," she said unable to stop smiling as she locked her arm with his.

"Merry Christmas," Hassan said leaning in kissing her.

Papo watched as they walked towards the yacht and boarded. He couldn't help but admire how good Rhae looked. He secretly regretted not getting with her that night in the club. Hassan had scooped her and was now sporting her like she was the queen of Nile. That bothered Papo more than he cared to admit.

"This nigga really sporting this bitch around like that," he mumbled to himself as he followed a group of guests boarding the yacht. "She a skeezer, I coulda had her," he said trying to convince himself. "I ain't want that bitch tho."

As he entered the boat he was immediately greeted by Hassan, Rhae and a mystery woman.

"Yo, Papo, this Rhae's sister Charlene," Hassan introduced them. "Make sure she have a good time tonight," Hassan said and nodded his head at his boy.

Papo gave her the once over. Charlene was definitely a beautiful female. The recent weight she had put on had her ass poking out the outfit she was wearing. She smiled at Papo, seeing him admiring her and her curves. It made her feel good to have a handsome and paid nigga like Papo checking for her. She had dollar signs in her eyes and was instantly attracted to him.

"What's up shorty," Papo said smiling at her showing off his gold bottom teeth.

"Hey," Charlene said with lust in her voice and eyes.

Papo gave Hassan the nodded as he put his arm around Charlene and walked toward one of the tables.

Hassan noticed the look of apprehension across

Rhae's face and tried to ease her mind.

"She in good hands with Papo. He'll take good care of her," he said. "She look like she like him too," he said charmingly placing his arm around Rhae's waist and walking her to their table.

For the next four hours the group sailed around the Hudson River enjoying dinner, an open bar and live entertainment set to the backdrop of the Manhattan skyline. Partygoers were seated at tables organized by the drug spots they worked at with the spot managers at the heads of each table. They enjoyed steak and shrimp and all the Moet they could drink all courtesy of Hassan, who spared no cost to make sure everyone enjoyed themselves. The crew was on top, no one amongst them was starving. He made sure of that and they all loved him for it and had pledged their loyalty to him. At the party, Hassan gave away over a $50,000 in cash, Rolexes and even a custom designed car to top members of the crew. He gave away trips and more cash to pitchers and others that worked in spots that bottled up all the crack the team sold. Up and down the ladder of his organization he treated everyone equally and showed love.

It was Rhae's first time witnessing Hassan as the kingpin she had heard so much about. She wasn't naïve at all to what it was that he did, but for the most part he kept it away from her. When they were together he wasn't the king of the streets or the CEO of a crack enterprise, he was just Hassan. But she was truly impressed by how people reacted to him and how much he was adored. He held her hand in his under the table for most of the night and she felt as close to him as she had ever been. He wasn't the bad guy some may have seen him as. No one saw the sides of him she had seen. All night she watched as he did things for others and as the boat was preparing to dock, she leaned over to him and kissed him on the cheek.

"I got something I want to give you," she said reaching in her purse. She pulled out a black rectangular box and handed it to him. "Merry Christmas."

"What's this?" Hassan asked surprised by her unexpected gift.

"Open it and see," she answered.

Hassan placed the box on the table, then placed his ear next to it, listening for a ticking sound.

"Oh my god, stop playing," Rhae said hitting him in his arm playfully.

"Just saying," he teased with a wide grin before

picking the box back up. Opening it he was momentarily blinded by the gleam of the massive gold loin head piece with ruby eyes and a diamond in the mouth. Hassan lifted the heavy piece out the box and saw that it was attached to a solid gold chain. "This is dope," he said leaning over and kissing her.

"Put it on," she instructed as Papo, Charlene and the other top members of the crew seated at the table looked on in admiration.

Hassan stood to his feet and slipped the chain over his neck. It was perfect and looked like it had been made just for him.

"That shit is fresh B," Birdie shouted from across the table.

"Hell yeah," Vel joined in.

"Yeah that's real nice," Charlene said looking over at Rhae nodding her approval.

"It's fly but what's the lion head about?" Papo asked.

"King of the jungle," Rhae said looking up at Hassan with loving eyes.

"Ha," he said.

Papo just stared at them both, jealousy and envy running all through his bones. It was slowly eating him alive and his budding habit wasn't helping.

Hassan was everything he wanted to be and had everything he wanted for himself, including the love of the streets and the woman on his arm. It was no longer enough for Papo to be part of the team. He wanted to be the star. In order for that to happen Hassan needed to be removed from the throne. The friendship they shared meant less than the power he possessed and Papo wanted it and he was willing to kill to get it.

As the boat docked and the partygoers began exiting the yacht, Charlene approached Rhae and Hassan and told them she was leaving with Papo. Hassan just chuckled to himself, he knew his boy had made an impression on her and he was about to unwrap her for Christmas.

"Be safe," Rhae said grabbing onto Hassan as she walked, feeling the effect from the glasses of champagne she tossed back all night.

Papo didn't even bother saying anything to Hassan, instead offered only a head nod as he pulled his car up and waited for Charlene to get in. Hassan was too wrapped up in his own thoughts to see the dirty look on his man's face. Instead, he couldn't wait to get Rhae back to the hotel room he had gotten for them and peel her out her clothes. Little did he know the dynamics of his friendship had changed with a single boat ride. Papo was his now his enemy, a snake in his grass just waiting for the chance to strike. Charlene hugged Rhae and trotted to the passenger side and got in. Papo slammed on the gas and raced out the parking lot and up the Westside highway.

"You ok?" Hassan asked a tipsy Rhae.

"I'm just fine, Hassan," she said attempting not to sound drunk.

They walked to his car and he opened the door for her, helping her inside before closing the door and jogging around to the driver's side quickly trying to get out of the cold. As they cruised up the Westside highway Hassan looked over at Rhae, who was staring out of the passenger window. The look on her face told him she had something on her mind.

"Everything cool?" he asked.

"Yeah," she stated unconvincingly.

"What's wrong?" he asked seeing through her lie.

"I want to ask you something," she said. "What do you see me as?" she questioned.

"Meaning?" a confused Hassan replied.

"As in what is my place in your life," she stated being as straight forward as possible.

Hassan took a deep breath; this was the moment

he knew was coming. Rhae had actually fooled him by holding out longer than he thought. But he was fully prepared for her line of questioning. "Your place in my life is right where you are now. Right by my side for as long as you want to be here," he said.

"For as long as I wanna be here. What about you?" she asked. "How long do you want me here Hassan?"

"I don't deal in forever Rhae, cause I ain't never seen shit end happily ever after where I'm from. I can only speak on the here and now. And right now, we here and I'm enjoying it. And I want it to last as long as it can," he said honestly.

Rhae respected his answer and felt the same way. She didn't believe in fairytales either. She had experienced all the coldness and harshness the real world had to offer. They were both alike in that way and was probably why she felt so connected to him.

"I only asked that because I want to know what happens after all this," she said. "After all the cars, the money, the trips and the Christmas parties. What is your escape plan Hassan?" she quizzed. "This life don't deal in *forever* either," she said thinking about Shank. "I've seen this life destroy good men and make evil men worst. I don't want that to be you," she said wholeheartedly.

159

"Like I said Rhae, I can only speak on the here and now. This is who I am right now, I can't think about later. I got a lot of people that depend on me right now. I got niggas out here trying to get at me right now. I ain't got time to think about the future," he said.

The two were so wrapped up in their conversation that neither of them noticed the van that sped up the highway and was now riding on the side of them. The sliding door on the van slid open and a man holding a fully automatic Heckler & Koch opened fire on their car.

Bullets rained down on the Ferrari, ricocheting off the bullet proof exterior. Rhae screamed in shock unaware that no bullet would penetrate the interior. Hassan shifted gears, pressed down on the gas and easily zoomed off from his would be assassins, switching lanes and exiting the highway at full speed. They had no chance of catching him and once they were in his rearview, he knew he was out of harm's way.

"What the fuck is going on Hassan!" Rhae screamed at the top of her lungs, rattled from the attempt on their lives. "You bout to get me killed out here fucking with you!" she yelled.

"Chill the fuck out!" Hassan shouted. "Calm

down."

"Calm down? Somebody just pulled up on the side of us on the highway and started shooting!" she yelled. "The highway!"

"I know," he said. "I know," he repeated lowering his tone seeing that she was shaken. He unknowingly put her in harm's way and felt terrible about it. "I'm sorry, I promise you whoever is behind this will pay for disrespecting us," he said grabbing her hand, squeezing it. "I ain't ever gonna let shit happen to you," he reassured Rhae.

The look in his eyes told her he meant every word he was saying and her heart melted. She felt like Bonnie to his Clyde, he was everything she wanted in a man and she knew than that she was in love with him. But what should have been a joyous feeling only left her more confused, questioning herself and torn on the inside. The life he was living wasn't going to end well and she knew it and the feeling she felt in the pit of her stomach made her nervous for him. Rhae had to find a way to save Hassan from himself. If they had any chance of being together in the future he would have to leave the streets behind. She stared out the window holding back tears as they rode through the streets of Manhattan on their way back to the

Bronx. Their romantic night in the hotel was ruined by the near death experience.

CHAPTER FOURTEEN

Rhae's beeper had been going off all day long, each time it was the same code. She knew exactly what it meant and hated the feeling seeing the number in her pager gave her. She pulled up in front of a luxurious high rise in Manhattan and parked. Unknown to anyone, Rhae was deep undercover, building a case against one of the biggest drug gangs in the city, MCM. But after the close call the other night followed by the urgent pages, she knew this meeting wasn't a good thing. She entered the building and rode the elevator up until she reached the 34th floor, than knocked on the door of apartment 3410.

The door slowly swung open and a thin light skinny woman, with black, shoulder length hair and several strands of grey mixed in stood in the door way.

"Come in Agent Price," the woman said coldly before turning and walking towards the living room of the lavishly decorated apartment overlooking the city. Special Agent Henderson's cover as Rhae's landlord called for decidedly better living arrangements than what Rhae had received from the bureau.

"So what is it that you wanted to see me about?" Rhae questioned trailing behind the woman.

"Have a seat," Agent Henderson instructed stopping in front of large mirror in the living room and checking herself out to make sure she looked flawless and not a hair was out of place. After 15 years of service in the FBI, she was enjoying the luxurious accommodation she had been provided to keep up the appearance. The look of disappointment on her face as she turned to look at Rhae said it all though. It had taken the young agent too long to respond to her pages and she was pissed. Agent Henderson hadn't laid eyes on Rhae since she had went to visit her after the trip to Atlantic City but last night's assassination attempt had her feeling as though Rhae might be in over her head. On the surface it seemed like the newbie agent was the perfect person for the job. She was street smart, beautiful, young and from the same blocks as the dealers she was chasing. She was a star student at the academy, a little rough around the edges but perfect for undercover work. Agent Henderson took a personal interest in Rhae, since she was once the young black female agent in the bureau. She wanted to help her as much as possible, something she didn't have earlier on in her career. She felt personally responsible and looked out for her mostly through tough love.

"What took you so long?" she asked but didn't wait for a response before continuing.

"This is unacceptable," she fumed as she took a seat across from Rhae and looked her in the eyes. "The MCM case has become a little too dangerous for my liking and I've decided to pull you out," she informed her.

"What!" an upset Rhae jumped to her feet. "Why? Why now I'm this close to closing the case," Rhae said.

"You were almost killed the other night. I can't place my agents in situations like that. I have a responsibility to you as your superior officer,"

Henderson said. "And personally I don't think you're ready for this assignment just yet. You may have bitten off more than you can chew. So I'm pulling the plug."

"I knew what I was signing up for when I took the job. I don't need training wheels and I damn sure don't need a babysitter," Rhae barked. "This is my case and I'm gonna see it through," she declared. "If not you can have my shield," she said tossing her badge onto the coffee table.

Henderson stared at Rhae, the veins bulging out the side of her neck as beads of sweat formed on the tip of her nose. That happened whenever she was angry. Henderson appreciated the passion she was showing, little did she know it had nothing to do with closing the case. Rhae was in deeply in love.

"I can appreciate your dedication to the job. I need more agents like you around here. If I did, I could really make a dent in this war on drugs," Henderson bragged. "So fill me in on where you are at on the case. What have you learned?" she asked as she got up and strolled across the living room over to the floor to ceiling windows.

"Well I haven't learned much about anything as of yet," Rhae answered untruthfully. "I haven't seen anything that has made me think that Hassan is who we think he is."

"There are bodies poppin' up all over the Bronx and Manhattan connected to MCM business and you are telling me he isn't who we think he is?" Henderson turned sharply and faced Rhae.

"That's the thing, if he is, he's very smart about how he goes about his business. I have never seen any drugs around. None, not anything, even as small as a joint. He's too smart for me to just bat my eyes at him, smile and think he is gonna lay out his entire operation to me."

"Yeah but I see you are enjoying the spoils of being a drug dealers girl," Henderson snidely replied. "I see the new earrings and other jewelry, not to mention I been receiving calls from the higher ups about a candy, apple red BMW."

"Isn't that what you wanted?" Rhae asked upset by the fact the bureau had been watching her so closely. "You want me to get close to him, gain his trust right? Be his girlfriend, than bring him down."

"The bureau wants results, not some know it all newbie riding around in expensive cars, paid for by a drug dealer."

"Oh excuse me, you're the only one that get to

living it up a little," Rhae said looking around at the beautiful apartment. "Only room for one queen bitch at the bureau!" Rhae shouted.

"Excuse me?" Henderson said taken back some by Rhae's disrespect.

"This is supposed to be a deep undercover assignment, no wires, no surveillance and especially no tails. But you've had someone following me?" Rhae said pissed at the lack of trust being shown to her. "If that's the case than pull me out like I said."

Agent Henderson exhaled deeply and walked back over to the couch and sat down. "Listen Rhae, this case means a lot to a lot of people, we just don't want any slip ups," she explained. "Heads will roll if there is."

The government had a hard on for Hassan and all of the drug organizations popping up around the city. War had been declared on the crack game. New York's Rockefeller drug laws were already the toughest in the country but after President Reagan signed the Anti-Drug Abuse Act the year before things only ramped up. The new act established a 100-to-1 disparity in punishing crack cocaine offenders compared to those caught with the powder form of the drug. A law aimed directly at the young kingpins getting rich in the black community. They had already taken down crews in Brooklyn, Queens and Manhattan and now they shifted their focus uptown. Hassan was in the government's scope and they were more powerful than any enemy he had faced on the streets.

"I know, I just think we've been wrong about how we've been going at it the entire time," Rhae explained to her supervisor but truth was she had been compromised. She had developed real feelings for Hassan while pretending to be his girlfriend and now she needed to stay on the case. At least until she figured out a way to offer Hassan a way out. She felt guilty about lying to him but what was she supposed to do. It was part of the job and came with the territory. She could have never imagined falling in love with him. But she was and felt compelled to give him a life line, a way out of the drug game. Hassan was all G and she knew walking him into the federal building and offering him a deal in exchange for his freedom wasn't even a possibility. He would laugh in her face, plus the powers wouldn't go for it in a million years. They were out for blood. Rhae saw herself as his only option but in order to save him she had to risk all that she had worked for. There would be no turning back from what she was about to do but it wouldn't be the first time she crossed the line or broke the law for someone she cared about. Rhae honestly had begun to question if she had made the right choice. Maybe she was on the wrong side of the law. She felt like an outcast amongst her fellow officers. She related to Hassan and understood him. She too thought like the dealers she had been trained to catch and put away. Her natural street sense made her feel like a snitch working against Hassan more than a cop out for justice. Rhae was a conflicted soul.

"What do you mean?" Henderson asked not understanding where Rhae was coming from.

"I don't think Hassan is who we think he is. I think he is just the face of the organization, a figurehead so to speak. A front for someone bigger behind the scene," she said making it up as she went. "I think I'm close to figuring out exactly who it is. I just need a little more time. I've slowly gained his trust and his guard has started to come down. I believe I can get him to tell me who is behind it all. Who is MCM's supplier. That would be a bigger get for the Bureau and strike major blow in the war on drugs. Don't you think?" she said feeding her captain line after line of bullshit, knowing it would appeal to her longing to look good to the higher ups.

"Yeah that is big," she quickly agreed. "Great fuckin' work Price. But I don't know how much longer I can hold my bosses off. They have already been chewing my ass out. We have spent a lot of money and time on this investigation. I need results and I need em fast. I will not be made to look like the fool if this doesn't play out like you said. Your ass will be on the line, do you understand me?"

"No problem," Rhae assured her than turned to leave. Her heart felt like a black college band was in her chest and it was halftime. Her emotions were all over the place and her nerves were shot. She had just put her career on the line for love. She prayed she was making the right decisions, but truthfully she was unsure both ways.

"Rhae," Henderson called out stopping her as she got to the door. Rhae heart skipped a beat as she paused before turning to face her fellow agent. "Don't forget this," she said tossing the badge Rhae left on the coffee table.

Rhae caught it and nodded, then exited the apartment in a haste.

Charlene danced around Papo's bedroom in just her

panties as the R&B music blasted out of the sound system in the house. She was on cloud nine and high out of her mind. She and Papo had been locked in the house for the past two days smoking crack and having sex. The thick cloud of smoke in the room and smell of crack and sex made the air unbreathable for any normal person. But it didn't seem to bother neither one of them.

Rhae had no idea about Papo's tendency to indulge in the crack cocaine. If she had, she would have never allowed Hassan to introduce the two of them. Papo had become more and more depended on the drug and had decided to get high before having sex with Charlene the night of the yacht party. He saw her eyes light up when he introduced the drug into the equation and thinking he was turning her on to something new but he had unknowingly released her old demons. Now he was the one being turned out by a veteran addict with a high tolerance for the drug. Papo had never binged smoked before and Charlene had him spiraling deeper and deeper into addiction by the minute. The more they smoked the more they craved each other and vice versa. They hadn't even opened the shades in the house or answered the phone. They were in crack heaven.

Papo sat up on the bed with his back against the headboard watching as Charlene held the pipe to her mouth, taking another hit. She felt like she was walking on air as she glided across the room to the rhythm of the music. Papo had smoked so much, he was numb and he felt like he couldn't get higher but it didn't stop him from chasing the high. After a while he started to grow agitated by the care free fun Charlene seemed to be having, enjoying her high while he was unable to obtain the feeling he was looking for. He opened the nightstand searching for more crack, only to find that they were out. That only seemed to enrage him further and fan the flame he had brewing inside. He stood up off the bed and walked over to Charlene, who was planets away on a high like no other. She sashayed over to him singing Keith Sweat's Make It Last Forever and attempted to blow him a shotgun. But he would have none of it. Out of nowhere Papo slapped her across her face, dropping her to the floor instantly.

"What wrong wit you?" Charlene cried out holding the side of her face as her high quickly vanished.

"Bitch you think I stupid," Papo shouted at her. "You think I'm stupid. You holding out on me. Where the rest of the stash?" he asked her glaring down at her with a crazed look in his eyes. "You hiding shit from me bitch," he said grabbing her by the throat and lifting her up off the ground. "I know you hiding shit," he stuck his hand in her panties and felt around until he found what he was looking for. Charlene had stashed a few vials of crack in her panties. Papo snatched them out and threw her back to the floor. He picked the crack pipe and lighter up off and sat at the foot of the bed and took a blast. "I see everything bitch, you can't fool me. I'm a supreme being," he bragged. "A bitch like you is lucky to be in the God's presence."

Charlene looked at him smoking and craved a taste. She wiped the small amount of blood leaking from the side of her mouth, and then crawled over to him.

"Yeah bitch crawl for the God," he said starting to stroke himself. "I run this town. Hassan is just in my way."

"You right daddy," she said going along with him. "That nigga ain't got shit on you," she egged him on, feeding his egotistical thoughts.

"I'm the reason niggas in the streets know that the crew ain't no joke. I'm the one out her putting my murder game down," he spoke out loud, no longer talking to her but to himself. "I should be the one they are talking about in the streets. I'm the star," he said.

"Yes you are," she said slowly kissing on his thighs working her way up. "Why don't you just kill him?" Charlene asked.

Papo grabbed her by her face roughly. "Fuck is you talkin' bout bitch. That's my man," he said blowing smoke in her face. "You talk too fuckin' much you know that?"

"Then you should shut me up," she said seductively.

"You a crazy bitch," he said then stuck his tongue in her mouth kissing her passionately. "But you might be on to something," he confessed though he had already decided he was going to kill Hassan anyway. He saw the look in Charlene's eyes and realized she could be of some use.

"Behind ever great man there is a strong woman," she said trying to secure her position as she seen him preparing to make his move to the top. She longed for that feeling again when she was on Shank's arm as his queen. That was the life she dreamed of and she saw Papo as her way back.

"Yeah but you have to prove to me that you're

worthy," he said to her.

"How do I do that?" she asked licking the head of his dick then taking him into her mouth.

"That's a start," Papo said as he laid back on the bed enjoying the head.

CHAPTER FIFTEEN

Rhae watched from her window as Hassan bopped up the sidewalk to the door of her apartment and rang the bell. She was so confused to what it was that she should do. She hadn't gotten a wink of sleep all night, tossing and turning in bed questioning herself and the choices she had made. There was no perfect ending or solution to her problem, either way someone was going to get hurt. Hassan was either going to jail or she was going to flush her career down the toilet trying to save him. It didn't seem fair to her. *Why?* she kept asking herself, not understanding why love had come to her this way. Her heart ached and her head was spinning. Hassan was the forbidden fruit but no matter how wrong it was, the heart wanted what it wants.

"Everything alright?" Hassan asked full of concern seeing the look on Rhae's face when she opened the door. Immediately he reached out and embraced her pulling her into his chest.

"What's wrong?" he questioned.

"Just one of those days, got a lot on my mind," she said honestly while still being vague.

"One of those days?" Hassan asked, seeing if she meant her cycle was on. He knew the mood swings would be in full effect if that were the case.

"No not that," she said somberly giving no reaction to his attempt at joking with her.

"So what is it then?" he pressed the issue now seeing she was so serious.

"Just still a little shaken by the other night," she lied trying to throw him off a bit. She wished she could just come out and tell him the truth. It was eating her up inside. She didn't want to lie to him but the truth was so ugly. How could she come out with the dirty secret she had been keeping? Hassan would probably put a bullet in her head right there in the middle of her living room. She couldn't blame him either, she knew the rules of the streets all too well. Shank had given her what amounted to a Master's degree in the game. Standing there she felt like a snake, disrespecting everything she was supposed to be standing for, at least the way Shank taught her. Up until than Rhae never had second thoughts about becoming a federal agent. Her only concern was bettering her life and finding stability after such a turbulent start. But Hassan had come along and reminded her of who she really was deep down inside. The "her" she was trying to run from and cover up with a badge and gun. The Rhae that was dressed in all black in the alley, the one that sought out revenge on Fats after all these years. That is who she was. She had been groomed to be the perfect ying to a real niggas yang. Rhae knew more about the game than most men and would be an invaluable asset to Hassan's rise to power.

"I know. I can't stress enough how sorry I am for putting you in danger like that. It will never happen again. I promise," he said kissing her on her forehead then on her lips.

Rhae felt the electricity racing through her body as she kissed him back. No one had ever made her feel like he did. She slid her tongue into his mouth and pressed her body up against his as he cuffed her booty. She was prepared to break all the rules for him and wanted to give herself completely to him, at least for one night. There was no telling what the future held for either of them but tonight she wanted to be his woman, not just play the role. It went against everything the bureau stood for, an agent sleeping with a suspect would taint the case but Rhae no longer cared. Hassan had her heart whether he knew it or not and she was about to give him the rest of her.

Rhae slid her tongue passionately in his mouth interlocking them in unison, the minty taste in his mouth made it even more inviting. Hassan welcomed her aggression by pressing her body against the window. She sat on the ledge and immediately reached for his belt buckle.

Hassan came out of his shirt in one swift motion, grabbing the back of her head and continued kissing her. "You don't know how much I want you," he said in between breaths.

Rhae took in his words with pleasure as she removed her shirt and tossed it. Hassan unsnapped her bra with one hand. Impressed with the effortless way he undressed her, Rhae grabbed his manhood in her hands and stroked it like it belonged to her. She wanted to feel him, be one with him, if only for this brief moment in time. Hassan moved with precision. Slowly he inserted his rock hard pole inside of her, making sure she felt every inch of him. The air was caught in her lungs as the blood rushed to the bottom of her feet as she received the pleasure given to her. Hassan was sized to perfection and Rhae gripped him like she was geometrically designed for him. Her moans grew louder as his thrust became harder, giving anyone looking out their window a memory for a lifetime. Hassan sex game was on point. He stroked Rhae until her body quivered in his arms. They went from the windowsill to the bedroom, never losing the stroke or interrupting their rhythm. Their mind and bodies were completely in sync and they enjoyed every minute of it.

CHAPTER SIXTEEN

The moonlight seeped through the slightly separated curtains in the bedroom and left slash marks throughout the room from the mini blinds. But it was the sound of the beeper vibrating across the nightstand that woke Hassan up out of his sleep. He slowly eased out the bed trying not to wake Rhae. Still the satin sheets slipped off her, exposing her from her back down to the crack of her ass. Hassan peeked over his shoulder at her sexy caramel body lying there peacefully. It took everything in him not to crawl back in bed and make love to her again. He picked up his cell phone and walked over to the window dialing

Papo's number.

Rhae rolled over and propped her head up on her hand, staring at Hassan like a high school girl would a crush. He was so sexy. She wished he would come back to bed. Now that she had a taste of him she wanted more.

Hassan felt her eyes watching him and turned to face her as he held the phone to his ear, waiting for Papo to answer. He smiled at her. He had never felt the feelings he was experiencing with Rhae. He hadn't been looking but love had found him. She was the other half that completed him. He wanted her next to him on the throne.

"Yo, what up B," he said into the phone hearing it pick up on the other end.

"Peace God," Papo said on the other end. "Yo, I got some info for you about that shit on the highway," an overly excited Papo said. "I found out where this nigga King Tito lay his head, so we can go see about him."

"Yeah," Hassan said eager for the chance to get some get back for niggas coming at him, especially with Rhae in the car. "Where you at now?" he asked ready to get to it.

"I'm in the hood, at our old spot on the roof," Papo said.

"Bet, I'll be there in a few," he said before hanging up.

Hassan turned and looked out the window taking a deep breath. The war in the street was really taking a toll on him. He was a leader of men and it bothered him that he had lost some of his comrades in the pursuit of the throne. No matter how much money he made, it wouldn't bring them back. He was from the biggest city in the world, filled with the biggest dreamers and he might have been the biggest dreamer of them all as a child. And he had reached heights never thought possible. He had united the projects and was sitting on more money than he knew what to do with. It made him think back to something Rhae had asked him on Christmas night. "What's next?" It was a good question, but one he had no answer for. All he had ever done was hustle to hustle, the game gave him a rush. The pursuit of money was all he knew. Drugs weren't only addictive to the people who used them, they were also addictive to those that sold them. Hassan was hooked on the game harder than the addicts he served.

Rhae saw the stressful look on his face and could tell he had a lot on his plate. She felt a similar weight on her shoulders. Rolling out of bed and easing up behind him, she rested her head against his back and wrapped her arms around him. "Where you going?" she asked in a soft tone.

"I gotta go meet Papo," he said not wanting her to worry about his real reason for having to leave. "But I'll be back soon."

"I want you to stay," Rhae pleaded sliding her hand down his chest into his boxers trying to persuade him. Hassan's manhood began to harden, she wasn't playing fair tempting him the way she was. "I love you Hassan," Rhae let the words roll off her tongue, while thinking it in her mind. But it was too late to take it back. It was out there.

Hassan turned to face her. He believed her because he felt the same way. "I love you too," he replied than kissed her passionately. "I been thinking about what you said. I'm a street nigga Rhae, it's who I am. The streets is all I know. I've never thought about leaving the game," he said honestly watching the hope in her eyes disappear as she lowered her head disappointed. He lifted her chin with his hand, so that she could look him in the face. "Until now," he continued.

Rhae felt her heart flutter. For a moment she allowed herself to get excited by the possibility. The feeling quickly disappeared at the realization that she still had to break the news to him that she was the feds. "Hassan," she said inhaling deeply and exhaling trying to calm her nerves. "I...," she started but Hassan beeper went off again, interrupting her.

"Let me go take care of this and I'll be back, then we can finish talking/.I promise," he said kissing her on the forehead. Stepping around her, he picked his clothes up off the floor and began getting dressed.

The loud knocking at the door woke Rhae up out of her sleep. She looked over at the clock to check the time, only 20 minutes had passed since Hassan had left the house. "Damn I nodded off that fast," she thought to herself as she rolled out of the bed. Hassan had really worked her body over, sexing her over and over again and she was exhausted. "He must've forgot something," she mumbled walking down the hallway towards the door. "Who is it?" Rhae called out in a hoarse tone.

"It's me Rhae, Charlene," the voice came through the door full of urgency.

"Charlene," Rhae repeated out of pure surprise then quickly unlocked the door. Rhae's eye grew wide and round when they landed on her friend. "Oh my god," she said covering her mouth in shock. To Rhae's dismay Charlene had slipped back into her old habits. She looked like she hadn't slept for days, her hair was unkempt and her clothes a mess. She had dark circles around her eyes and her lips were white, crusty and cracked. Rhae's heart broke into pieces looking at her.

"Hey Rhae," Charlene said rocking back and forth, the jones getting the best of her. She needed another hit to calm her nerves. "Can I come in?" she asked realizing she was still standing out in the hallway.

"Of course," Rhae spoke almost in a crying tone, as she tried to remain strong for her sister. Rhae had so much on her plate at the moment that Charlene relapsing was the last thing she needed. But she swore by their friendship that she would help her no matter what. She looked at Charlene and noticed she was still wearing her clothes from the night of the Christmas party. I should've never let her out of my sight, it was too early, she thought to herself.

"Rhae I need some money," Charlene pleaded standing in the middle of the living room.

"I need to get high, please."

"No I'm not giving you any money Charlene. You're high enough," Rhae scolded her.

"Please Rhae, please," Charlene begged as she

grabbed onto Rhae. "This is it, I promise. I just need one more hit. Then we can go back to the rehab. Just let me get high first."

"No!" Rhae shouted pulling away from her. "This shit has to stop and it has to stop now," Rhae demanded. "You are going back to the rehab tonight," Rhae said turning her back and walking over to a desk where she kept important papers. She began searching for the number of the treatment facility.

"I'm not going anywhere," Charlene roared.

Rhae heard the hammer of a gun cock back and turned to see Charlene pointing a .38 special in her direction. "What are you doing?" Rhae questioned her with disappointment in her tone and on her face.

"I'm proving my loyalty to my man," Charlene boasted proudly.

"What are you talking about?"

"Papo, my man. He's about to be the new king of the streets and I'm going to be his queen. He's tired of living in Hassan's shadow and I'm tired of living in yours," she declared. "You always got treated better than me. I had to do all type of shit to make sure we were straight while we were in the streets. I protected your lil' ass. Kept you from getting beat up, raped and all type of other shit. I'm the one that had to fuck niggas so we could eat. Even with Shank, I had to lay on my back to keep food in our stomach but who got treated like she was made of gold, you, Lil Bit!" a furious Charlene shouted.

"Don't you dare speak Shank's name," Rhae said pointing her finger at Charlene. "You left us both high and dry when we went away. We were all supposed to be a family. When was the last time you even been up to the jail to see him?" Rhae asked.

"Family my ass, bitch," Charlene said. "Shank was a come up, that's all… nothing more, nothing less. I didn't love him and I still don't. It was all about the money for me, sorry to bust your bubble. Shank can rot in hell for all I care. He can't do shit for me or nobody behind bars. It's a new day, it's all about me and Papo," she said. "Right now he's meeting with Hassan's ass and he is gonna put a bullet in his fucking head. Then the projects and the crew will be his," she confessed.

"You think the rest of the crew is seriously gonna go for that? You saw the type of love and respect they have for Hassan. Nobody is having that. Papo could never be half the man Hassan is," Rhae said feeling a fire burning inside of her at what she was hearing. "Why do you think I picked Hassan?" she asked. "I could've had Papo. I met them on the same night but he's not built for the throne. Any woman, not desperate enough could see that," Rhae said trying to hurt Charlene feelings.

"Yeah right," Charlene said firing the gun barely missing Rhae.

"Don't do this Charlene, please," Rhae waved both of her hands in front of her pleading with her friend. "You are high out of your mind. You don't want to do this. Not for him, he is not worth it. You don't want to go to jail for killing a federal agent," Rhae confessed.

"You lying bitch," Charlene said. "You're not a fucking fed. I know you, remember."

"I'm not lying let me show you," Rhae said slowly reaching under the desk and feeling for her badge. She removed it and showed it to Charlene. "See, I'm not lying Charlene. I'm undercover, I have been this whole time. I'm building a case against the MCM. They are all about to go down, don't let Papo take you with him. Let me help you," Rhae begged.

Charlene couldn't believe what she was hearing. "A fed...a fucking fed," she said to herself still pointing the gun at Rhae. She was so confused staring at a crying Rhae. Charlene didn't feel the same emotions for Rhae though, her thoughts were all selfish ones.

She thought to herself that if she killed Rhae for Papo, it would really prove her loyalty, especially knowing now that she was the feds.

"I'm sorry Rhae, but I have to do this," Charlene said lifting the gun and pulling the trigger.

Rhae dove to the floor barely missing being shot. She reached under the desk where she had pulled the badge from, snatching a gun and firing two shots, all in one motion. Both shots hit Charlene directly in the chest, piercing her heart, killing her on impact.

Rhae jumped up from the floor and raced to put on some clothes. She had to get to Hassan before he met with Papo. He was walking right into a trap and didn't know it. Tears ran down her face as she thought about him being set up. She needed to get to him fast. She grabbed her gun and keys and raced out of the apartment. When she reached the sidewalk, she heard sirens, saw flashing lights and unmarked cars pulling onto to her block in front of her apartment building. Rhae didn't know what was going on until she saw Special Agent Henderson exit one of the vehicles. The agent wore a stylish pants suit and shoes with her badge swinging from a chain around her neck. She approached Rhae, shaking her head as a few other agents stood idle in the background.

"Agent Henderson, we need to locate Hassan. I just received information that he's being set up to be killed right now as we speak," a frantic Rhae spoke.

Agent Henderson saw the look in Rhae's eyes and it was then her suspicions were confirmed, Rhae was in too deep. She had feeling for Hassan that went deeper than anyone could imagine. "Agent Price," Henderson spoke somberly. "It's too late, Hassan was murdered tonight." She broke the news to Rhae.

Rhae felt her knees get weak and it took everything in her not to collapse to the ground. She wanted to breakdown and cry right there but didn't want her superior officer to see that she had been compromised by the case. "What?" she asked. "What happened and how do you know?" she asked hoping with all she had that Henderson was wrong.

"I heard it for myself," Henderson said. "The lion head piece I gave you to give him had a listening device planted in it. I heard everything that happened tonight. Everything," Henderson expressed, letting it be known that she knew Rhae had crossed the line. "But that's nothing for you to worry about, I'm the only one who knows," she told Rhae tossing her the tape. "I would destroy that if I were you," she offered her advice. "But I was able to capture Hassan and

Papo's conversation on the roof and heard the moment he was killed."

Rhae no longer able to take it, she quickly wiped the tears that had begun to fall before the other agents saw it.

"Papo has the chain," Agent Henderson informed Rhae. "So I also was able to hear him make a phone call setting up a meeting with someone named El Jefe. They are meeting tomorrow. It sounds like he is making his move to fill Hassan's shoes. I think El Jefe is the man behind it all, the supplier, the one you were talking about. We're going to raid the meeting and arrest everyone. Hopefully we can catch them red-handed."

"I want to be a part of the team that goes in," Rhae declared. "I want Papo to see my face and I want to see his when he realizes I'm the one responsible for bringing him down," Rhae fumed needing to get some sort of revenge against him for killing Hassan. "There is a dead body in my living room," Rhae told a shocked Henderson. "I'll explain it all to you on the way to the office," she said as the two women walked to one of the unmarked cars.

CHAPTER
SEVENTEEN

"I must admit, you were the last person I expected to hear from," El Jefe greeted Papo wiping the corners of his mouth with the cloth napkin. He was seated alone at a table in a half empty restaurant enjoying a meal, flanked by a few of his henchmen who stood while he ate.

"I figured we have such a good thing going with you, if it ain't broke why fix it," Papo replied. "I don't see any reason why we can't continue doing business."

"And how do you think Hassan would feel about

that?" El Jefe questioned.

"No disrespect but Hassan is no longer here, so his opinion no longer matters. But as his closest and most trusted friend, I think he would want me to continue building on what he started. That is why I'm here, I'm in charge now and I hope we can make as much money together as you and him did," Papo said standing in front of the table.

El Jefe sipped his drink while never taking his eyes off of Papo. He could see the hefty size bags under his eyes, the sunken in face and the jittery mannerisms. Papo read like an addict, standing there sweating for no reason. El Jefe didn't trust him, even though he had no weapon when his henchmen patted him down and he wore no wire, Papo was bad business. El Jefe could never do business with someone as unstable as Papo appeared standing in front of him.

"You know why I've lasted so long in this game, my friend?" he asked rhetorically, continuing before Papo could speak. "I've always trusted my gut. And my gut is telling me you are not good for my business. See unlike my late friend Hassan, I could never trust a strung out junkie muthafucka like you," he said.

"You got it all wrong Jefe," Papo pleaded his case.

"You can trust me," he said. "You would make a ton of money with me."

"All money ain't good money," he replied. "How'd that work out for Hassan?" El Jefe asked bluntly. He had suspected one of Hassan's own men in his death but it wasn't until Papo called that he knew for sure who was responsible for his death. "I had a lot of love and respect for Hassan," he said. "And it would bring me great pleasure to see whoever was responsible for killing him pay."

"Me too," Papo said refusing to look El Jefe in the eyes.

"I'm glad we agree," he said nodding to his henchmen who grabbed Papo restraining him. El Jefe stood up, grabbing a knife off the table and walking over to Papo placing the sharp blade to his neck.

"Nobody move, FBI!" one of the waiters screamed pulling his gun.

El Jefe looked around, to his surprise all the waiters on the floor had drawn their weapons and had them surrounded. Every staffer in the place was an undercover agent. He looked at Papo seething. "You fuckin' rat bastard you set me up," attempting to push the knife deep into his neck, only to be stopped by one of the agents.

"No he had nothing to do with it," Special Agent Henderson said as she strolled into the room. "Even though he led us right to you, he had no idea we were onto him," she said slapping cuffs on El Jefe as other agents cuffed his henchmen. "Isn't that right Agent Price?"

"Exactly," Rhae said as she entered the room with a menacing look on her face heading straight for Papo.

His face hit the floor seeing Rhae in the FBI jacket with her badge hanging around her neck. "This bitch is the feds?" Papo asked in disbelief. "Hassan was stupid for trusting you. You might've had his nose open but I never trusted your ass," he shouted. "I should've put a bullet in your fuckin' head you fed bitch," he threatened.

"You have the right to remain silent, use it," she replied before reading him his rights and slapping the cuffs on him. When she was finished she turned him around to face her. As he spun around the gleam of the lion head he sported around his neck caught her eye. Rhae felt a lump form in her throat making it hard for her to swallow. Looking closely, she could see it was slightly dented, the result of being hit by a bullet and still had specks of Hassan's blood on it. Tears formed in her eyes as she stared at the medallion. She reached out and snatched it off Papo's neck.

"You don't deserve to wear this, you fuckin' snake," she said then spit in his face before storming out of the restaurant.

Papo just laughed. "Fuck you bitch, you're no better than me," he shouted at her back as she disappeared through the door of the restaurant.

Rhae hopped into the driver's seat of her squad car, tossed the chain onto the passenger seat and slammed the door shut. She let out a loud scream followed by a flood of tears, all her penned up frustration coming out at once. Rhae's heart ached immensely. She hurt for herself but mostly for Hassan he died for all the wrong reasons. He loved all the wrong people including her. No one in his circle was who they said they were or who believed them to be. His loyalty took him straight to the grave and Rhae couldn't help but to feel partly to blame. She had no excuse, she had a job to do and she couldn't even execute that right. She wasn't an addict like Papo, she wasn't dependent, she had a choice and she placed herself in his life to witness his being taken. Nothing right came out of it. She thought seeing Papo in cuffs would give her the closure she so desperately sought but it hadn't.

CHAPTER EIGHTEEN

ONE YEAR LATER

The torrential downpour made it hard to see more than a few feet away, making driving an almost impossible task. It had been raining off and on for the past few days but this was definitely the worst of it. Most had decided to play it safe, staying off the roads and remaining dry in the comfort of their homes. Rhae was one of the few that had no choice but to brave the elements as she commuted back and forth to work. She had recently been relocated to the bureau's Philadelphia office and was living just outside the city in the bedroom community of Cherry Hill, New Jersey. Normally a half hour commute but the weather conditions added an extra 20 minutes to her ride. Rhae exhaled a deep sigh of relief when she turned into her subdivision, happy to finally make it home. It had been another long day at the office and she couldn't wait to enjoy a long hot bath, a glass of wine and snuggle up under the covers. The rain would provide her with the perfect soundtrack to sleep. Rhae turned into the driveway of her beautiful new three story townhome and hit the button opening her garage. Pulling in she cut off her engine, grabbed her bag and exited the car.

Rhae's breath got caught in her throat and the pace of her heart quickened as she saw what could only be described as a ghost emerge from the darkness. Rhae couldn't seem to speak and her knees became weak as she stared in the face of a man she thought was dead.

Damp and cold, it was no telling how long Hassan had been lying in wait for Rhae to get home. But his intentions were quickly made clear as he lifted the gun he held in his hand and pointed it at her. The look in his eyes was one of pure hatred, something Rhae had never seen before from him. To her he resembled the grim reaper.

"Hassan," she finally was able to speak. "I thought you were dead," she said as her lips quivered and she was on the verge of nervous breakdown. The emotions running through her body was overwhelming and her chest became tight. For a moment Rhae thought she would go into cardiac arrest from pure shock.

"I just need to know one thing," Hassan said as his voice cracked and tears ran down his face as his grip tightened on the gun. "Was any of it real?" he asked. "Or was it all part of the job?" Gone was the love he once felt for her, replaced by hate and anger. She had betrayed him. But for his own selfish reasons he needed to know the truth. While the world thought he was dead, he had watched from a distance following the trial that took down his entire MCM crew and El Jefe's organization. Hassan read newspaper clippings of testimonies and saw pictures of Rhae on the stand. He watched her become a media darling as the bureau paraded her around as the agent who brought down one of the biggest drug rings in the city. The Rhae he saw in the newspaper wasn't the woman he knew and fell in love with. The feeling of betrayal cut so deep with him, he spent the past year trying to track her down. Now he had finally come face to face with the woman responsible for the heartbreak he felt, dealing with her lies and deceit.

"Hassan just let me explain," she pleaded.

"Answer my question!" he raged waving his gun at her.

"Hassan..."

"Answer the fucking question Rhae," he said quickly moving closer to her and pressing his gun to the middle of her forehead.

The feeling of the cold steel frightened Rhae. "It wasn't in the beginning," she admitted truthfully. "But I swear to you Hassan, I never lied to you once when I told you I loved you."

"I don't believe you," he said as tears rolled down his face. He never hesitated in the streets when pulling the trigger. The slightest bit of doubt and he could have easily been the one being filled with slugs. But this was different, he had allowed this woman into his heart like he had never done before with any other person. His love for her was real, even if hers wasn't. His finger was twitching as it rested on the trigger of the gun. Killing her would give him the revenge he was seeking but staring at her, his heart wanted him to grab her and pull her into his arms. He was confused and conflicted. Hassan had a broken heart and a tortured soul.

"Please, I'm not lying to you. I loved you with all my heart. I cried so many nights after I thought you were gone. I felt guilty for deceiving you. I felt sorry for you. Nobody in your life was who they were supposed to be. Not Papo and certainly not me. I felt like a piece of me died with you," she spoke. Her words were sincere, she spoke from her heart hoping that it would thaw the icebox in his. "I wanted to tell you I swear, I just didn't know how. I didn't want to lose you, but I ended up losing you anyway. I was trying to figure out how to get us both out. I was just too late. But I promise you, there is not a day that goes by that I don't think about you Hassan, I still love you with every part of me," she said through tears streaming down her face like the rain outside.

"How am I supposed to believe anything you say? Everything you ever told me I have to question. You lie for a living, it's what you are paid to do," he said. Deep down inside he wanted nothing more than to believe her. He wanted her to convince him not to kill her. He wanted to love her the way he once did.

"I don't know what you want from me. I can't

change anything that happened. All I can do is tell you how sorry I truly am. Whether you believe that or not it's up to you but I need you to know that I truly did and do love you Hassan, I can't die with you not knowing and believing that," she said pouring her heart out. "Let me show you something, please don't shoot," she requested reaching inside her bag. "I kept this as a reminder of you, I take it everywhere I go," she said.

Hassan remained silent as he watched her pull out the gold chain with the lion's head attached to it. Looking at the chain that saved his life, sent chills up his spine and through his body. He could still see the dent in the medallion, from where it had taken the brunt of the bullet meant for his chest. It would have struck him directly in the heart killing him instantly. He ran his hand over his chest feeling the scar that stretched from his chest to his stomach. Hassan felt lucky to be alive, even the bullet to his stomach had missed all his vital organs. His mind and heart was at war. Rhae's betrayal called for her death, it was the rules of the street, he knew it and she knew it. But love is a powerful thing and seeing that Rhae had held on to the chain meant a lot to him. Hassan just stared at her, she was more beautiful than even he remembered. She was the woman who he had actually contemplated leaving the streets behind for. He loved her that much. Truth was he still loved her that much, it was that love that had made him track her down. He had convinced himself that it was revenge that he sought but deep down inside Hassan was seeking redemption. A second chance at what had escaped his grasp the first time around. He was already presumed dead, that meant he and Rhae could go anywhere and start anew. Hassan had assumed a new identity and with the money he had stashed away he would be able to live comfortably for a while. The more he stared at her the more his anger subsided and finally he lowered his gun.

Rhae threw her arms around him and they began kissing passionately. Their chemistry was undeniable as they both became flooded with old emotions. Rhae's heart fluttered like it always did around him. She was on cloud nine, loving Hassan was all she had wanted and now she had a second chance. She was overjoyed, the excitement caused her body to release endorphins to her brain, producing a feeling of euphoria.

Boom!

Rhae's euphoric ride came crashing down as she

felt a burning pain in her stomach causing her to stumble backwards as the gold chain in her hand dropped to the floor. When she looked down she saw the crimson blood stain growing larger by the second. Rhae looked Hassan in the eyes not believing what he had just done. She placed her hand over the wound and blood began to seep through her fingers.

Hassan looked her directly in the eyes, the menacing look he had in the beginning had returned. Revenge had one out. He loved Rhae with everything in him but she had betrayed his trust once and he couldn't risk her doing it again. His weakened heart couldn't go through that. In his mind she was just a great actress playing a never ending role. He could never truly trust her. Everything they had was built on a lie and she was a master manipulator, a professional deceiver. Hassan believed in the code of the streets and she was no better than a snitch to him, so she had to be dealt with. Showing love had almost got him killed and he wasn't about to make the same mistake twice.

As Rhae collapsed to the floor, Hassan heard the sound of a baby crying coming from the backseat of her car. He looked down at Rhae then walked over to the car and opened the back door. What he saw sunk his heart. A beautiful baby boy was strapped into a car seat, screaming at the top of his lungs. The gunshot had startled him out of his sleep. Hassan unstrapped and picked him up, holding him close to his chest. He didn't have to ask, looking the little baby in his face was confirmation enough but he still needed to hear it from her. He walked over to Rhae who laid on the floor of the garage gasping for air and kneeled down next to her.

"Is he mine?" he asked.

Rhae, barely able to speak, just nodded her head as a single tear escaped her eyes and ran down the side of her face.

Hassan began to cry realizing what he had just done. "I'm sorry, if I would've known," he said only to be interrupted by her.

"It's too late now," she whispered shaking her head slowly as more tears dropped and her chest heaved up and down slower and slower.

"No Rhae please don't die on me. I'm gonna get you some help. Don't you have a radio in your car, I'll call for help," he said. "Please just hold on," he begged.

"It's too late Hassan," Rhae said as the cold feeling invaded her body. "He is your responsibility now, promise me you will take care of our son," she said reaching out and grabbing Hassan's hand and squeezing it with the little bit of strength she had left.

Hassan couldn't believe the turn of events that had just taken place. "I promise you Rhae, I promise," he said through tears and snot running from his nose. "I love you and I'm sorry about all of this," he poured his heart out to his dying love. "Thank you for him," he said looking down at his crying son laying against his chest. "I got him, don't worry."

"I know," she said. "I love you both," she forced out the words as she began spitting up blood.

The sight of her coughing up blood only made Hassan cry harder. "What is his name?" Hassan asked realizing he didn't know his own son's name and time was slipping away.

Rhae didn't immediately answer as she was extremely weak and felt the life leaving her body with every breath. Finally, with her dying gasp, she was able to utter the last words she would ever speak. "His name is Rheason."

"Rheason," Hassan repeated looking down at his beautiful son, a perfect mixture of both his parents and cracking a smile. But the rush of joy he felt suddenly was replaced by more grief when he felt Rhae's grip on his hand go limp. Looking down at her, he could see that she had expired. Although her eyes were still open, there was no life left in them.

Hassan just sat there crying and rocking his son back and forth in his arms, taking in all that had occurred. He used his hands to close her eyes then leaned over kissing her one last time. He looked down at his son once again then back at her lifeless body. He had made a promise to her and he planned on keeping it. His son wouldn't have the chance to know the beautiful woman his mother was or experience the amount of love she had for him. But Hassan swear that he would tell him all about her when he was old enough to understand. Hassan had lost his mother to the streets long before AIDS took her and he had now cursed his own son with the same motherless life. The guilt he felt was unmatched but his love for his son and the promise he had made to Rhae gave him the strength he needed to go on. Rising to his feet, he covered Rheason's head with the blanket he was wrapped in, then they both disappeared out the garage into the darkness and rain.

THE END...FOR NOW

ABOUT THE AUTHOR

Raised in Peekskill, NY, Ty Marshall is an undeniable talent with a highly skilled pen. Discovered by New York Times Selling Authors Ashley & JaQuavis, his ability to seamlessly weave authentic depictions of the street with great storytelling sets him apart from the pack. He is widely considered one of the rising African American authors in the country. Ty has independently released several titles which include: Keys to the Kingdom, 80's Baby and Eat, Prey & No Love. He also released a ebook through St. Martins Griffin entitled Luxury & Larceny. Ty is a proud husband and father that currently resides in Atlanta, Ga.

www.tymarshallbooks.com

www.ingramcontent.com/pod-product-compliance
Lightning Source LLC
Chambersburg PA
CBHW031331170626
46807CB00002B/650